PRAISE FOR *THE BLUE VALLEYS*

"These powerful stories ring like bells. They are about our mothers and fathers, our land and rivers. They are about us. They map our hearts."
—Clyde Edgerton, author of *Where Trouble Sleeps*

"This outstanding collection of short stories is award-winning poet Morgan's first work of fiction. . . . Morgan has a deft touch for the nuances of family ties, and his characters in this realistic, evocative, and often lyrical collection are formidable and well drawn.
—*Publishers Weekly*

"Morgan, an acclaimed poet, here turns to fiction in a collection of thirteen short stories all set in the southern Appalachians and all told with a vibrant lyricism. Spanning eras from Civil War prison camps to modern trailer parks, these tales brim with fetching characters, men and women, young and old, all more or less haunted by their Blue Ridge Mountain ideas and attitudes."
—*Denver Post*

"Stunning . . . and every page has something beautiful on it."
—*San Jose Mercury News*

"Robert Morgan is a fine poet with five books of poetry to his credit. With *The Blue Valleys,* his first collection of short stories, he proves that he is a fiction writer of grace and talent. . . . All of these stories are excellent. Morgan is an outstanding writer whose works should be widely read."
—*Orlando Sentinel*

The
Blue Valleys

A Collection of Stories

ROBERT MORGAN

SCRIBNER PAPERBACK FICTION
Published by Simon & Schuster
NEW YORK LONDON TORONTO SYDNEY SINGAPORE

SCRIBNER PAPERBACK FICTION
Simon & Schuster, Inc.
Rockefeller Center
1230 Avenue of the Americas
New York, NY 10020

First Scribner Paperback Fiction edition 2000
Published by arrangement with Peachtree Publishers, Ltd.

SCRIBNER PAPERBACK FICTION and design are trademarks of Macmillan Library Reference USA, Inc., used under license by Simon & Schuster, the publisher of this work.

Designed by Lisa Lytton-Smith

Manufactured in the United States of America

1 3 5 7 9 10 8 6 4 2

Library of Congress Cataloging-in-Publication Data
Morgan, Robert, 1944–
The blue valleys / Robert Morgan.
—1st Scribner Paperback Fiction ed.
p. cm.
1. Appalachian Region, Southern—Social life and customs—
Fiction. 2. Blue Ridge Mountains—Social life and customs—Fiction.
3. North Carolina—Social life and customs—Fiction. 4. Mountain
life—Fiction. I. Title.
PS3563.O87147 B57 2000
813'.54—dc21   00-032932

ISBN 0-7432-0422-0 (Pbk)

For Lamar Herrin and Michael Koch

Acknowledgments

Epoch: "Night Thoughts"
St. Andrews Review: "War Story"
Appalachian Heritage: "Family Land"
Maryland Review: "Let No Man"
Celery: "Blinding Daylight"
Jacaranda Review: "A Brightness New and Welcoming"
(as "Camp Douglas")
South Dakota Review: "1916"
Memphis State Review: "The Half Nelson"

The author would like to thank the National Endowment for the Arts and the New York Foundation for the Arts for grants which were of great help in the completion of this book.

Contents

A *Brightness New and Welcoming*

"HERE JOHNNY, have a swallow."

The two South Carolinians held the wooden bucket between them, and the orderly drew out a dipperful and held it to his lips. John took as much into his mouth as he could, hoping the quantity would cover the muddy taste. The only water on the island came from a well in the corner of the yard, a hole not more than twelve feet deep and covered with boards. The boat coming over from Chicago brought a keg of water for the guards and officers, but the prisoners had to drink from the well.

"Better drink it up Reb; all you'll get for a while."

The Sandlappers moved on with the heavy leaking bucket. John couldn't tell if the taste of the water was worse than the smell of the camp. He held the wetness on his tongue a few more seconds and forced himself to swallow, then lay back on the cot. The canvas above was completely still. There was no sun, but no wind either in the hazy heat. It was so humid the lake itself seemed to have risen and filled the air with a viscous stench. How could it be so hot this far north?

"Better drink it up Reb," the orderly said two or three tents away.

It was the spring he thought of most often, of the trail down into the hollow, and the rocks he had put at the lip of the pool. The water boiled out from under the root of the great poplar. For that high on the ridge it was a bold spring. When he found it, when he was looking for land to buy across the line in North Carolina, there was a muck of leaves and sand collected around the head. And he dug it all out, dug a channel for the overflow to move the run-off quickly so the little swamp hardened and grew grass. And he shoveled out the basin back to the roots of the poplar and the pores from the mountainside. There were at least three fountains coming together, and as the basin cleared he saw the sand dance above the inlets. He gathered a pail of the whitest sand from the branch and spread it on the floor of the pool, and rimmed the edges with rocks. On the hottest days of July the water was cold when he came down from the cornfield. It tasted of quartz rock deep under the mountain. Sometimes when he found a specially brilliant crystal he would place it in the spring to sparkle for all to see. Spring water was touched by all the mineral wealth it had passed through, the gold and rubies, silver and emeralds in the deep veins. The water was a cold rainbow on the tongue.

And he built for Louise a washstand in the meadow just below the spring, a puncheon table where she could place her tub and washboard, and wring out pieces before spreading them on bushes to dry. He brought the cauldron up from North Fork in the wagon and placed it on three rocks high enough to keep the fire underneath.

"You put that thing close to the spring," she said. "I ain't breaking my back carrying water to wash for you men."

"There's only one man here."

"There will be more. I'm thinking ahead."

He cleared out the brush on the side of the hollow and leveled out a bench for the washstand. He'd seen women use stumps for the washing or bend over tubs set on the ground. But Louise was already showing her condition. It was easy to chop the young poplars on the south side, and to grub up the woodsfloor. Within a year they had worn a regular path to the spring, and to the washpot. And the ironweed and goldenrod and Queen Anne's Lace sorted themselves out in the meadow he had cleared.

On a hot day, coming into the hollow from the bright field, you couldn't see much in the shade at first. A few mosquitoes and deerflies in June and July made the air seem needled, and the rocks wet the knees of your pants when you knelt to drink. As you put your lips to the surface of the pool and sipped, or scooped the gourd into the scattered reflections, your eyes adjusted, and you could see the sand and quartz on the bottom like beacons on a plain. Tiny spring lizards gripped the deepest floor, and the pores under the root were ebullient and busy as ever. It was like watching an hourglass that never ran out of grains, a source feeding tirelessly as time, the flow running long before he ever saw or bought the acres and long after he left them. Nothing made him feel the vastness of time as much as the spring. It seemed the dial of some instrument. He looked into its depths and at the reflections on the surface. He stayed so long looking into the cold lens he had to mask his embarrassment when Louise came up behind and said, "Don't you ever get enough to drink?" and he had to turn back to the blinding sunlight and work.

But he had lost track of his memories. Sometimes he thought he was back home after the war, and sometimes he thought he had deserted again and was hiding out at the spring. In the cool mornings he watched the mist on the creek valley below as he walked out to milk in the wet grass and stopped between the gap and the spring to listen to the bobwhites call.

THEY WERE COMING AROUND with the bucket of oatmeal. The same two Sandlappers carried it and the orderly ladled out the porridge in cups. At least they called it oatmeal, though there were husks mixed in, and shells of bugs and fly wings, all hard to tell apart. And the mess was watery and unsweetened. It seemed to make his dysentery worse.

"This one stinks so bad I hate to go by him," he heard one of the Sandlappers whisper.

"Tarheel can't help his stink," the other said. "Besides, he won't eat."

John could no longer smell himself. When the fever first struck he could sniff his heated skin; the flesh seemed to be cooking on the bones and the outer layers dying. His hands smelled like meat that had been half boiled and was sweet with first decay. But all the sweating, all the diarrhea, the vomiting, left no scent in his nostrils. The nerves in his nose had been burned out. If only somebody would wash him.

But he had no money, and the orderlies left him alone except for the drink of water twice a day, and the cup of oatmeal or soup.

"Hey Powell, what time is it?"

It was Woodruff in the next tent. They had emptied out his own tent except for him, but Woodruff was still in his, only six or seven muddy yards away. Before he got too weak he and Woodruff had talked across the space. Only Woodruff knew he had the watch still. They had an agreement. If the orderlies knew about the gold timepiece it would long ago have been gone. It was all he had left.

He reached under the cot where the watch was tucked into the rags. He would have to think of a new hiding place because they might clean up the rags there any day. The metal was cooler than his hand. He listened again. The Sandlappers with their bucket were four tents away. He brought the dial close to his face and called, "Eleven-thirty."

Woodruff didn't really care about the time; he just wanted to talk, wanted to know if he was still conscious. The doctor came around only once every day or two now, which meant they had given up on him. The doctors attended those who might recover. All they really knew how to do was amputate. The saw was their favorite instrument. They had taken Woodruff's arm, and now he was getting stronger. But he had seen other cases, both on the field and in the camp, where some boy begged them them not to cut, screamed he'd rather die than be a cripple. And they held him on the table and poured the morphine down him. And when the boy woke he cried for days and said he still felt his leg rotting out in the ditch where they had thrown it.

There were things he wanted to tell Woodruff again, about how you reached Mountain Page by the Buncombe Turnpike and Saluda Gap, about the trail up to his place by the Red Old Field. He wanted to tell him again about the spring. He couldn't remember how much he had told him before. Maybe he had told him everything already, or maybe he had just thought about it and was remembering the intention. All this had happened before, and he had thought about it before. He was too weak to talk now.

A bell rang somewhere. And there were shouts and a whistle. He concentrated hard to remember where he was, to visualize the tents of the hospital section of the camp. He was number four on the seventh row. There was nothing but mud and rotting canvas. And beyond the sick area was the yard where all the others lived, with puddles here and there full of urine and excrement, rotting rags. Most of the refuse had been thrown there when the yard was frozen over, and when thaw came the depressions filled and turned putrid. No one would wade in to clean them out. The island was so level there was nowhere for water to run, without ditches to the lake. And the prisoners were too weak to work or care. When they arrived in early winter they hoped for rest and warmth and regular rations, after the long train ride north, after the starvation of the battlefield. The cattle cars got colder as they crossed Kentucky and Ohio, Indiana, Illinois, each night more freezing than the last.

When they stopped to exercise in a field, around a bonfire, he was too stiff to take a step, and the guard prodded him to circle the fire with the rest.

"Johnny too lazy to walk," he joked.

There must have been five thousand on the island. In the early months they gathered for prayer meetings and singings on the frozen ground, and clapped and stamped the ice to keep warm. The wind off the lake could knock you down. They sometimes crawled to the well, and had the water blown out of the bucket before they returned to the tents.

"ENLIST NOW and receive a bonus," the handbills in Saluda said. He told Louise he would take the bonus and serve his term. Everybody said the fight would be over in six months, at most a year. And the bonus would buy the fifty acres of adjoining land which the Nixes were willing to sell.

He walked to Hendersonville and signed on, at the tent in front of the courthouse. And Louise cut his uniform from homespun and dyed the material with butternut in the pot behind the house. He had his picture made in Hendersonville, holding the Bible over his heart.

"I'll be back in time to put in crops next year," he told her, when she stood with hoe in hand by the young corn. "You'll have to carry through this year but I'll be back in the spring."

And he walked down the trail and up the road in his new uniform, carrying a duffel and a blanket, and biscuits with sidemeat for his lunch.

And for the next six months he walked and drilled, he rode on trains. He waited in the sun, and slept on grass, in tents, in cold wind. He ate the hardtack and potato gruel with bits of meat floating, and he cursed the mud and march up the Valley of Virginia, and down the Valley of Virginia. Across the Rapidan and the James, along the Potomac, he marched and waited. Once the men said they could see the dome of the Capitol in the distance, but all he could see was a wisp of cloud to the east.

The letter from Louise began, "Dere husbun John, it raned all thrue the fall, but I saeved most of the corn. The babye wannt come till March." By then the fighting looked different. It seemed the Yankees would not give in no matter how hard General Jackson whipped them. By Christmas he was studying on his foolishness for enlisting. While lying on the frozen ground, or shivering on sentry in the long star-covered night, he thought of his cabin up the branch beyond Mountain Page and Louise by herself milking and carrying a sack to mill. Her people lived just over at Saluda Gap, but her brothers had all joined. He'd seen her brother Mem once after a battle and they were so happy they danced and slapped each other's shoulders before the marching took them apart.

Through Christmas and New Year's he studied, and knew it was dangerous to think so much of what he'd left. It was no good to hanker. It made him careless on sentry and careful in battle to stay behind others if possible, loading and reloading.

He would not have thought it could be so cold in Virginia. He had seen men shot for stealing a ham from a smokehouse they passed, and others hanged from trees along the road for deserting to go home at Christmas. They were an example, the general said.

Through the long days of February, the long days by the sour fire, the nights in the pitiful tent, he studied on his bed at home, and Louise there by the fire waiting for the baby. He was trapped, he was helpless to escape, this far from home and without money. He didn't even have a map for getting back to Carolina, and it was too dangerous to confide plans, to ask for directions.

A warm day in March decided him. A breeze crept out of the south smelling of new grass and fresh plowed ground. He thought of Louise with a baby and unable to break the fields and put in a crop. He had promised them the one year. That night when he went out to stand guard and was relieved he just kept on walking. By dawn he was forty miles to the west. He walked up the Valley of Virginia, past burnt-out farms, up the James River, sleeping in cowsheds, shooting squirrels until his powder gave out.

And walked into the yard one evening at milking time and knocked. Louise was feeding the baby and looked up in terror, pulling her shawl down over her shoulder as he stepped in. For the country lived in fear of the outlaw gangs. And she didn't recognize him behind the beard, the shrunken features.

"I thought you was an outlier," she said. "I prayed you would come, now that it's corn planting time."

NEVER HAD HE BEEN so happy and so scared at once. Though the place was back up the hollow a mile from any road, he still feared working in the fields in daytime. No telling who might pass and report him. Only family could be trusted, and sooner or later the Home Guard would come looking.

The horse was startled the first morning he hitched her up for plowing while it was still dark. There was frost on the grass, and the faintest light in the east. The stars were still out as he creaked with the turning plow down to the potato patch. There was a heavy stubble because Louise had not cleared the fields of stalks in the fall, and he did not want to burn the acres and call attention with the smoke. As he broke the ground he had to keep clearing away the stalks that gathered on the plow's tongue and shaft. Whoaing and starting again he turned perhaps a third of an acre before the sun came up over Callahan. He ran a couple more furrows before unhitching the plow and heading for the shed. He'd leave the horse in harness and perhaps Louise could plow a little after breakfast to cover his work in case it was noticed.

But because they had no money and would have nothing from the garden until July, and because he knew he'd have to leave sometime for the army or prison, he started cutting tanbark. The tanning yard in Tryon was still working and the sap was just now in the chestnut oaks. His oaks were on the highest land on the ridge, and every day he took the ax, after plowing and planting before dawn, and vanished into the woods. If the Guard came looking what could they find, his pipe, his clothes, his baby? Let them search.

Tanbark was a one-time crop because the trees had to be cut to be peeled. Once the trunk had been felled a skilled peeler could ring the bark with the ax every three or four feet and shuck off sleeves and curling strips of the skin. The inner bark was sopping wet with sap. That was the part the tanners wanted. When they got a wagon load of bark they crushed it in their mill and than soaked the pulp to leach out the tanning acids. It was that steeped water they bathed the leather in for months, sometimes half a year.

John worked quickly, knowing he had only a few days before the sap had lost its prime and the first leaves came out. He was still weak from the long walk back from Virginia, and his hands blistered from the ax. Sometimes his fingers cramped so he could not let go the handle after chopping and flensing off the bark for hours. When he had to rest he sat down in the leaves, listening to the silence of the woods, a crow calling from somewhere in the hollow, a robin in the cucumber trees. He thought of his unit still fighting in Virginia. He lived every day as though this would be his last summer on the place.

At night he dreamed he was still in the army, and was hoping there would be bread and grease in the morning. He wished he were closer to the fire. And woke with Louise beside him, and the cabin warm, and knew it was time to hitch up the horse.

Already things were getting scarce in the stores. The price of salt had risen a hundred-fold. People were digging up the floors of their smokehouses and boiling the dirt to get the salt drippings, then boiling down the water for a cup of dirty salt. Salt would soon be more valuable than its weight in gold, it was said. The price of leather had quadrupled, and with most shoemakers away in the army boots were no longer to be had. John wore his infantry boots until they cracked, and he patched them crudely with a piece of cowhide. Soon he would be going barefoot.

Louise continued to attend church, carrying the baby so no one would be suspicious. Once she hitched up the wagon and drove all the way to North Fork Church, to tell his Daddy and Mama he was home. It was at North Fork he had first seen her, when she walked with her sister down from their place at Saluda Gap on Sunday. And Mama invited them to stay for dinner. That afternoon he walked back up the long hollow through Chestnut Springs, seeing them home. By the time they got to the old Poinsett Bridge they were holding hands. At the place where the road started winding up the mountain face below the Gap they kissed in the shade of honey locusts. And before they walked into the clearing at the top of the mountain and were greeted by the Ward hounds they agreed to be married.

The next Sunday Mama and Daddy drove up to visit, bringing a bushel of potatoes and several moulds of butter. But their arrival must have aroused suspicion, for no sooner had they sat down to eat than four members of the Guard rode up into the yard.

"Here, Johnny, can you take a drink of this?" It was a large woman dressed in black bending over him. He raised his head slightly, and she poured from a bottle into a spoon and held it to his lips. The thick blackberry syrup felt sweet and hot going down his throat. Already flies were touching his lips to get the stickiness.

The big woman looked like his aunt Icy Mae. Suddenly he remembered who she was, Mrs. Atkins, "The Angel of Death" the prisoners called her, because she wore black and visited only those thought to be dying. Her husband had been killed in Virginia, and in her weeds she visited the camp each week to bring orange juice and syrup, sometimes candy and cakes, to those in the worst condition. Her visit to him meant the doctors had put him on the most critical list.

"May the Lord bless you," she said, screwing the lid back on the bottle. "All you need now is to rest. You have nothing to fear. Where are you from, Johnny?"

"North Carolina."

"I'm sure your family in North Carolina think of you often. You are ever in the care of God. Have you had a letter from them?"

"No."

"Next week when I come I'll bring pen and paper and write to your family. Are you married?"

Before she left she asked if his soul was right with God, and he nodded.

"God bless you, dear Johnny," she said, and moved on to another tent. The flies buzzed to his sweetened lips, but he was too weak to lick the last of the syrup away.

"Could you give Powell some morphine?" he heard Woodruff ask the doctor when he came around later.

"No, he's resting now, and there's no morphine to spare."

WHEN HE WAS SAVED at the revival John felt a terrible shame and conviction as he walked up to the altar, along the aisle lit by lanterns. The planks he put his face against were cold, and he prayed to be forgiven, to be accepted into the flock. But it was the way his tears wet the pine wood and made it smell of resin he was thinking of when Pastor Howard touched him on the shoulder and asked if he accepted Jesus as his personal savior. When he nodded the preacher took his hand and raised it and said, "Thank you Lord. We have a new brother."

When he stood he felt the relief flooding him, the faces of the Amen Corner and the choir accepting him. He felt lighter than he ever had, and assumed it was the burden of sin that had been lifted from inside him. And all that night, as everyone shook hands, and as he walked back home swinging the lantern, and as he lay in the loft listening to the katydids, he was at peace, and in a brightness new and welcoming.

But weeks later, and months later, when the brightness had faded, he wondered how it was he had changed. He was the same, thinking the same temptations, fearing and doubting the human way. "Once saved always saved," the Baptist preachers said. Had he really not been saved? He was the same John as ever except that he was now a member of the church and had been baptized in the pool at the bend. Was he an imposter? Had it merely been the approval of his mother, of the preacher and the congregation, he had sought?

The sergeant of the Guard was a Ballard from the Macedonia Church. Through the window John saw him dismount and walk toward the door. John put a finger to his lips, looked at Louise and Mama and Daddy, and climbed the rungs to the loft. He pressed himself against the cobwebbed chimney at the far end of the house by the time Ballard knocked at the door.

"Ma'am, we're looking for your husband. We've heard he's been hiding out."

Louise stepped back and the sergeant walked into the room, looked at the table with its extra plate, and inspected the corners. He climbed the ladder and looked around the dark attic from the top rung, as John pushed himself closer into the clay and rock of the chimney. Then Ballard lowered himself back to the puncheon floor.

"You tell John if you see him," he said to Louise, "You tell him the Law will go easy if he gives himself in. Otherwise he can be shot on sight by any member of the Guard as a deserter. You tell him hear?"

"You folks want to stay for a bite of Sunday dinner?" Louise said.

"No ma'am, we got duties," the sergeant said. "But we might just take a piece of chicken to nibble."

"Then I'll get a box."

"Won't be necessary," he said, and took the platter of fried chicken up and emptied the pieces into his hat.

"Do you want a napkin?"

"This will do just fine."

When he was gone they all sat around the table, Louise and his Mama and Daddy and little Emma, looking at the empty platter, and the bowls of beans and rice, corn and okra. They were still sitting there without reaching a fork when John climbed back down the ladder.

THERE WAS a clump of laurel on the slope above the spring. After Ballard's visit he was afraid to stay in the house in the daytime. And after the leaves had come out on the chestnut oaks there was no more tanbark to be peeled. When he finished his early morning work in the corn he retired to the little opening in the laurels he had made and furnished with a cot and blanket. There he sat most of the day, looking down on the spring, at Louise working over the wash table, little Emma asleep on a quilt. He sipped from his water jug and hoped it wouldn't rain.

And later, when the Guard came again, and again, and searched the loft, he retreated further up the mountain by day, and then met Louise at the spring at dark where she gave him a basket of bread and bacon, fresh corn. Sometimes they used the cot in the laurels, in the early evening, with katydids loud in the woods around and stars prickling through the canopy above. As they lay in the dark he knew he would turn himself in, as soon as the tops were cut and the fodder pulled.

"WOODRUFF," he was calling when he woke. "Woodruff!" But something was wrong. The last thing he remembered was the two Sandlappers and the orderly coming round with the pot of soup. But he had been too weak to touch a spoon or cup to his lips. He no longer felt the heat. It had turned cool while he slept, and the flies were gone. He could no longer smell the stench of the camp, the mudholes and privies, and the sewage from Chicago floating in the lake. He shivered and wished he had a blanket tight around him, over the scraps of dirty cotton. He wished he was by a fire. He could smell only his own fever and heated nostrils. It was a ripe cooking smell, as though he were baked and getting tender.

Something was wrong. They were in battle again and shells were going off, worse than the night he surrendered. Then the air was full of lead bees and the hiss of grapeshot. It seemed impossible that anyone could survive the air full of lead. When the Yankees appeared with their bayonets he raised his arms.

But it was wrong now, the shooting and bombardment. The air was lit, the filthy canvas, with red and green and yellow flashes. All seemed reflected on water, and on the hazy sky. One blast followed another. Maybe the Southerns had broken through in Tennessee or Virginia and run the Yankees all the way to Illinois, pushed them back into Lake Michigan, driving them to Canada where they belonged. Maybe the Federals were blowing up the city and its arsenals and powder magazines to prevent their being seized. Maybe they were blowing up the prison island. He didn't care about the war anymore.

The charges were getting bigger and brighter. He heard a bomb hiss in the water and then go off. It was so cold he jerked and thought he must be remembering the last battle. It was winter and he had been asleep a long time since the awful July heat and stench. A soldier was screaming some-where as they sawed off his leg, and then one of his arms, and cauterized the stubs with redhot irons that hissed and scorched as they touched the flesh.

He was so cold it must be December, and the war had reached such a desperate stage they were killing the prisoners by firing on the island from gunboats. If he had to die it was better to die in battle. The flames and blasts were many-colored. He must be hallucinating with hunger as he heard men did. It was only a matter of time before his tent was hit. Would the fire warm him? Would he be warmed by the flames of hell, in the lake of fire?

He didn't know what it meant. He had never known what it meant. Grownups and preachers and teachers and politicians acted like they knew what everything meant. And he kept thinking as he grew up he would learn too. And he thought once he joined the church it would be clear to him. But nothing was revealed, and he just kept waiting. And everything happened as it did, and he was still waiting for the explanation. He had forgotten the reason for all the men in mud and rags and dying, and the women at home digging up the smokehouse dirt for salt. And the questions from when he was young, of what he was doing alive anyway, and why he was himself and not someone else in another country and time, got pushed to the side, but were left hanging, like jobs still to be done.

Something was wrong, and he was tired and cold. And things had been wrong a long time, since he woke up and the firing was going on. Since he got sick and could no longer catch rats and seabirds for meat. Since he turned himself in after the fodder was pulled. Since he joined the Confederate army. It traced all the way back. Something had always been wrong. Something was wrong at the beginning of creation he guessed. It was in the nature of things that they were wrong. On the night before he left for the army he listened to the oaks muttering outside the window and the hush of the distant waterfall, and knew things were wrong.

"Woodruff," he called out again. And this time in the flame light from the shells Woodruff loomed above him and bent down closer.

"Woodruff, who's firing?"

"Speak louder Powell. Can you speak?"

And with every cell concentrating its energy he shouted, "Who's firing?"

"It's the Fourth of July, Powell. They're having fireworks in the city. And I heard a guard say they're celebrating the fall of Vicksburg and a Yankee victory at Gettysburg, in Pennsylvania. I stood out by the fence and watched the show over the water."

He wanted to tell Woodruff how cold he was, and where the watch was in the cot. But he couldn't tell if he was speaking or not. He heard himself say the words. Maybe he had already said them and was remembering what he had said. Or maybe it was just the memory of his intention to speak that he recalled. It was the timing that confused him.

That's the way it was on the train coming north, after he surrendered. It was cold and windy in Tennessee, but colder in the mountains of Kentucky. They huddled in their rags in the cattlecar. There was no room to lie down. He sat on the stinking straw and the car lurched and rattled and light sliced through the cracks stabbing his eyes. He leaned on one buttock till it got sore, and then the other. And his bones ached. It must be the ache of fever, or the numbness of the cold.

No one sang in the railroad car as they kept jerking and shaking north. Somewhere in Kentucky snow began to sift through the cracks and wet the straw under them. He was sure the cold in his nose and throat would become pneumonia. There was already a weakness in his breath.

As he drowsed and slept and woke through those long nights on the train, he began to be confused about what had already happened, and what he had merely thought about. He dreamed he had gone to the prison camp and was being returned at the end of the war. He thought of Louise and talked with her, and then remembered he was on the train. He thought they had arrived and were assigned quarters, and then he woke on the train, a white winter sun shredded through the cracks. He asked the man he leaned against if they were still in Ohio and the man said, "You asked me that two minutes ago, friend."

Every twelve hours they stopped the train and all were

ordered out to stand beside the tracks and relieve themselves in the weeds. He decided he would stay inside at the next stop and lie down on the straw. He was constipated anyway with fever and low rations. And then he couldn't remember if he had stayed inside at the last stop or just planned to at the next. Act and intention and memory were mixed up. In one dream he went into the weeds during a stop and ran off into the dark snowy woods looking for a lighted cabin where they would let him in. He even saw the inside of the cabin, the hearth where stew was steaming, the bucket of water in the corner. "Any child of God is a friend," the woman said when she opened the door. She held a nursing child. She was shorter than Louise. She fed him stew and he ate and drowsed until the guards knocked on the door and jerked him back into the cold. He wasn't sure but what it had happened and he had been pushed back onto the prisoner train. He licked his lips for some residue of the stew, and tasted nothing but his chapped skin and soot.

The cot shook and shivered and Woodruff hovered nearby. "Powell, can you hear me? Are you awake?" The cot trembled like the floor of the cattlecar. Maybe it was him who was shaking. He must give the watch to Woodruff. It was down there somewhere. It was solid and cold in his hand. Long ago Woodruff had said there was a letter from Louise that said she was fine except the outliers took all the corn he had grown and ran their horses over what they couldn't carry, grinding it into the mud. And there was a new baby named John. And it was too dangerous to live at the place before he got back, so she had returned to her family at Saluda Gap. But that was a long time ago. Or maybe in the future, or in a dream, when Woodruff read it to him as he leaned down close as he was now.

"Look what I brung you now," he said.

And in the bright light he saw the little bottle brought to his lips. The spiritous liquid chilled his tongue and warmed his throat as Woodruff poured in drop after drop. The drops soaked right through his tongue and skin and rose like vapor into his sinuses, and through his brain with an ether-like breath, like salve on a burn. And then the drops seeped down his spine and throughout his veins. Until the day was very bright and dark at once. He kept thinking of the row of sunflowers he had planted along the fence, and they were huge and bright, though he remembered them as black—bright and black. Woodruff was still talking even though he had stopped talking.

WHEN HE GOT OFF the train in Greenville he saw the station was still intact, but the building had been stripped of every bit of decoration and furnishings. The windows were broken in places, and some panes seemed to have been removed intact, for what purpose he couldn't guess. Many stores nearby were boarded up, and blue soldiers patrolled at every intersection. Little groups of soldiers stood around fires at each corner. It was cold in the April dawn.

Greenville did not seem to be the town he remembered. But then he had never spent any time there, usually driving through with a wagonload of produce for the Augusta river market. He and his Daddy made the trip every December when the hams were cured. There was a stillness, a deadness, about the town. But it was still early. A few people were out besides the soldiers. A negro chopped wood on a sidestreet he passed. It was all so quiet, so empty. The dogs he saw were showing their ribs.

"Hey, Johnny," a soldier called after him, but he kept on walking.

He was glad to reach the countryside and follow the red clay road north through green banks and new weeds in ditches. There were almost no horses or cows in the pastures, but many of the patches had been broken up.

In his soreness and weakness from the long train ride the road seemed to stretch out forever ahead, getting longer with each step. He hoped somebody would come along with a buggy or wagon and offer him a lift. He wished he had some money and could stop at a large house and ask for something to eat. They would give it to him for nothing, but he could not ask if he had no money in his pocket. He wished he had a uniform, and not the rags from the prison camp. He wished he had shoes for the rocky road bit into his feet.

When he increased his pace, the soreness in his lungs returned. The least stretching hurt. The pain had stayed with him long after the pneumonia that came in the long spring rains. For a week the lake water had lapped right into the camp and spread into the tent and under the cot. He stopped to cough, and rest on the bank.

A mockingbird seemed to be following him. He had heard it running through a medley of voices and saw its gray form and cocked tail in an apple tree above the road. And then it was sitting on a fencepost ahead as he approached. And later it was off in the oaks as he wound through the woods. It kept repeating a three-note theme, along with its other quotes and variations, following him for miles. Was it trying to tell him something?

By noon he reached the peach country at the edge of the hills. And though it was late for blossoms a few trees still shone and shivered above the red clods. They seemed like pools of sparkling water at a distance. He stopped several times to watch the petals in the breeze and rest his lungs.

Because he had gotten off the train so early he had gone eighteen or twenty miles. Should he ask the man plowing with a mule if he could stop and stay at his house? The tightness in his lungs was slowing him. Should he stop at the dust-covered house ahead and tell them who he was, hoping they'd invite him in? A cur with hackles raised greeted him at the side of the road, its eyes fixed on his. He walked on, stooping to give himself a slight advantage with his weight.

The road turned into the hills, and he saw the blue mountains above. They rose like smoke in the haze of the northern sky. I am rising a step at a time, he thought. Continuing like this, one foot after another, I could step into the sky, into heaven. A step at a time he could reach any height, and deep into the future. The thought gave him strength. The higher he got the newer were the leaves on the trees. On the mountain the grass was green but shorter. He was climbing back into early spring. The slopes were many shades of yellow and gold and faint greens. All sharps and flats, he thought. Women bent over washtubs by branches. Smoke from the cauldron fires rose above the trees. He saw apple trees blooming in the little hollows, protected from frost, and dogwoods further up the slope. And further still redbud and sarvis stood out like puffs of coral cloud on the higher ridges. A cowbell tinkled out of a cove, the music carried by a down-draft. He passed a smokehouse with a pile of dirt in front where the floor had been dug up. Once he smelled the scent of mash blown up a mountainside and realized someone had enough corn for making whiskey. The church at Mountain Page needed new shingles. Somebody had torn the door off the schoolhouse in the Old Field above the road.

It was late in the day but not dark when he turned into the trail. Some of the poplars were in leaf but the maples were just budding. It had been a late winter, and he could tell by the packed-down leaves in the woods there had been a lot of snow. The sweet-shrubs were just beginning to bud, but would not bloom for another month. He could look far down over the piedmont he had crossed, but the roads and hills were indistinct with distance. It was cool this high.

He stopped by the spring, fearing to see it was clogged with sticks and rotting leaves. But the pool had been kept clean, and the clear water thrust up from under the poplar roots and dimpled the surface like wrinkled silk. He took the gourd from its stick and drank slowly. The tart cold taste seemed to come from the deepest part of the mountain, from the beginning of the world. He had forgotten the living poplar taste and the quartz taste of mountain water. On the path by the wash stand he wiped the drops from his beard.

The yard in front of the house had been swept with a willow broom, and geraniums in boxes were blooming along the porch. There was a box of cabbage slips that had been wet down by the door. He felt the gold watch in his pocket as he knocked. A baby cried inside. The door was opened by a young woman whose hair had come down over her cheeks and neck. She held a baby on her hip. He bowed to her slightly, and pulling the watch from his pocket held it out to her. "My name is Woodruff," he said, "And I have brought you this."

Pisgah

WHEN THE BELL RANG inside the one room school, children emerged from both front doors at once, clutching their dinner buckets and shoving each other into the sun. It was the first day of the spring session, and the recent rains had left the playground goose pimpled, darkened here and there by puddles.

"Let's see where they go to eat," Carlton, the biggest boy, said to his friend James. Their eyes followed the new boy and girl who had moved to the side of the group. Most children sat on the steps in the sun, or walked down to the spring to open their lard buckets and eat dinner. The new boy and girl looked around them, as though hoping no one was watching, and hurried to the pines at the edge of the clearing.

"We'll follow them," James said.

"No, wait till they get their buckets open," Carlton said. "Then we can see what they've got."

Several of the others were watching Carlton now, while pretending to go about the business of eating. Having new students in the school was an important event, and they knew Carlton would not let the chance pass without some response.

The new boy and girl had gotten behind a pine tree before opening their pails. Carlton and James shuffled over to the edge of the clearing.

"What you all got to eat there?" Carlton said, stopping a few feet from where the younger children sat on the pine needles.

"My name is Nelse," the boy said. He turned slightly away from his interrogator. Both he and his sister had stopped eating.

"What is your name?" Carlton said to the girl.

"Mossy Bell," the girl said without looking up.

"You look like a mossy bell," Carlton said.

He and James laughed and moved closer.

"I can't tell what you're eating," Carlton said.

The boy on the ground did not say anything.

Carlton glanced back at the schoolhouse. During the lunch hour the teacher always sat at her desk eating from a brown paper bag and correcting assignments. Then at the end of the hour she came outside to the outhouse before ringing the bell again. She was not in sight, and several of the other children had moved over to the edge of the woods to observe.

"What do you think they are eating, James, lard or mush?" he said.

Carlton leaned over to look into the little girl's pail.

"Where you people from?" James said.

But neither the boy nor the girl answered. They looked at the ground.

"They're trash from up on Pisgah I bet," Carlton said.

Sun on the pine needles raised a sweet resiny scent. There was something sickening in the smell and the fresh breeze.

"They must be eating grits right out of the bucket with their fingers," James said. "Just sopping them up."

"Can't you all afford bread?" Carlton said.

A tear bulged in the little girl's eye.

The other children gathered closer, looking from time to time back toward the schoolhouse. Those who had gone to the spring returned, wiping their mouths on sleeves, and came over to see what was happening. The blue Pisgah mountains reared far above them.

"What kind of clothes is them?" Carlton said and pointed. The girl's black stockings had holes in them. The boy wore a coat that was too big and too heavy for the season.

"Is that your daddy's coat?" James said.

"Maybe it's his mama's coat," Carlton said.

"Maybe they ain't got no mama or daddy," Ulyss said, but Carlton looked at him, and he said nothing further.

"I bet they're Indians from up there on the mountain," James said.

"Hey, are you a big brave Cherokee?" Carlton said, and patted his lips in a war call. He danced around a few steps. There was snickering in the group.

"Can't we see what you got in them buckets?" Carlton said. "We're awful curious about what Indians eat."

Both the boy and the girl had put their hands over the pails. Neither would look up.

"I think they're eating cold mush," James said.

"No, it's just a dab of grease on bran," Carlton said. "Here, let's put some salt in it. It needs some seasoning." He began to kick dirt toward the buckets.

"And it needs some pepper too," James said, and he kicked dirt and pine needles toward the children.

Laughter ran through the group. Someone threw an acorn that landed on the boy's head.

"I'll bet they eat itch-rag stew," James said.

The girl began crying, her face in her hands over the bucket.

"Ain't you done enough?" Ulyss said.

Carlton turned and shoved Ulyss backwards, and then pushed him again. While the others watched to see if there would be a fight the boy and girl stood up and ran off into the pines, leaving a bucket lid on the ground.

"Hey, you forgot your dinner plate," Carlton called, picking up the lid and sailing it after them.

"Let's follow them," James said. But just then the teacher rang the bell.

"NELSE, we ain't got a bit of coffee," Mama said. "We ain't got coffee, and no money neither."

He was still in bed on the pallet in the loft above the fireplace. The quilt was wrapped tight around his shoulders, but the chimney was warming from the fire Mama had started below. He sat up and listened to the roof just above his head. The rain had stopped and the shingles were quiet.

"Is it snowing?" he said.

"No, it ain't snowing," Mama said. She bent over the fireplace stirring oatmeal. At least there would be something hot for breakfast. Nelse buttoned on his pants and climbed down the ladder. Mossy Bell was sleepy at the table, wrapped in one of Mama's shawls.

"George never would have let things come to such a pass," Mama said. "We never was out of coffee or money long as he was alive."

Daddy had gone off to the Confederate War and never returned. Nelse could not remember him, though he came back on furlough when Nelse was three.

"It's a pretty fix we've come to," Mama said, as she spooned out the oatmeal on the plates. Two things Mama lived for were tobacco for her pipe, and coffee. She had been out of tobacco for more than a week, and now the coffee beans were all gone. The hog meat had been used up by February, and most of the potatoes in the cellar. From now until garden time they would live on the oatmeal left, and grits and bread, and greens pulled on the banks of the branch.

"There's nothing on the place to trade," Mama said, as she sprinkled a pinch of maple sugar from the gourd on the oatmeal. She was indulging them with sugar because there was no coffee. All the chickens had been eaten or sold except two setting hens and the rooster. The cow was dry and due to freshen in a month.

Mossy Bell looked down at her plate and stirred the sugar into her porridge. She had talked less and less since they quit going to school.

"She'll talk when she's good and ready," Mama liked to say.

Nelse ate fast, burning his tongue a little on the smoking spoonfuls. This morning Mama was glaring at everything and he wanted to get outside as soon as possible. Bright sunlight sliced through the cracks around the door.

"It must have cleared," he said.

"You go on down to the store and see if Old Salem will give us something," Mama said.

"He said last time there wouldn't be any more until we paid," Nelse said.

"Well, you'll just have to pester him," Mama said. "Tell him we ain't got a bit of coffee."

As soon as he scraped the last of the oatmeal from the plate Nelse stood up to go. After the days of rain he wanted to get outside the house. And he did not like the way Mama glared at him this morning, as though she blamed him because the coffee was gone. The coffee had been getting weaker for several days, as the March rains continued.

He unlatched the door and stood in the blinding rush of early sun.

"Here, take this," Mama said. It was her silver thimble, the one Aunt Josey had given her before the war, when she married. "If Old Salem won't trade any other way get what you can for this."

"What will you sew with?" he said.

"I'll do," she said.

He ran out onto the cold wet ground. The rain had left puddles in the path down past the stable. A few weeds were just beginning to show green around the edges of the clearing where he had burned off the stubble last month. The cow was restless in her stall and he threw her a handful of tops before going on. Mossy Bell or Mama could bring corn and water to the hens and rooster.

The trail wound down to the spring and then on toward the cove. The air was so clear he could see through the bare oaks and hickories down valley where poplars and locusts were already budding green. Spring arrived weeks later up there than in the valley. People said no one should live this high above the creek, but Daddy had cleared his patch up here, and built the cabin, and Mama said that's where they would stay.

At a glance Nelse scanned the valley from the green at the lower end up to the lavender of the bare slopes and on up to the black of the balsam covered peaks. There was not another house in sight until the very end of the cove, halfway to Brevard.

How could he get Old Salem to give them any more credit? He felt the thimble in his pocket and shuddered with the morning chill and the wet ground between his toes. At least he was out of the house and the rain had stopped. He ran down the trail, banking on the turns and sometimes hopping from shoulder to shoulder over the worn track. A blue-jay squawked. Where the trail passed a little ramp meadow he thought he saw something flash into the undergrowth, and stopped to look closer. Great beads of water flashed wherever sun touched the wild onions.

Spots of sunlight mottled the leaves under the bushes of sweetshrub, and the leaves themselves were many-colored shades of tan and brown, bleached and pressed by the winter snow. Shadows and black rotting pieces of bark dotted the woods floor, and spoons of water standing in the few curled leaves. But something was there; he had seen it move.

Nelse stepped closer to the edge of the undergrowth. It was the eyes he saw first, the big wet agates between lashes, and then the fawn emerged from the dapple of the leaves and brush, so delicate and tiny it must be almost a newborn. Its legs were thin as his fingers, and it stood only a little taller than a cat. Its spots blended with the leaves.

He breathed out slowly. He must have been holding his breath for a minute. There were sweet shrubs behind it. Maybe if he edged up very slowly he could catch it.

As he eased closer the fawn did not move. Yet he imagined it was about to tremble in the cold morning air. Was the doe somewhere nearby watching him? Had the doe been killed or died when the fawn was born? A stick broke under his foot and the fawn blinked, but did not run. If he could get near enough he could leap and hold it in his arms. The bushes behind would prevent it from running in that direction. He paused, not daring to breathe. Another bluejay squawked above, and he waited for it to stop.

The fawn seemed to disappear and reappear as he watched. It seemed possible it might vanish into the forest floor like some vision, something he had dreamed. When he was a body length away he sprang, crushing a little sweet shrub in front as he went down. Only at the last instant did the fawn start, and almost jump over his left arm. But he caught the little neck and pulled the body to him. His chest hurt where the bush had gouged into him, but he ignored the pain and stood up, pressing the fragile body under his chin.

The fawn made leaping motions, and trembled in his hands, its heart fluttering against the tiny ribs. He felt something hot and wet down his shirt, and saw that it was a boy fawn.

Clutching the body to his dampened shirt Nelse ran on down the trail. He was warm now and sweating as he threaded the footlog and climbed a rise. He was concentrating so on the fawn in his hands he was almost at the schoolhouse before he noticed the cries of the children at recess.

Quickly he slipped off the trail and swung through the pine woods, staying behind the brush and trees. He made an even wider circuit around the outhouse, hoping no one had gone farther into the woods. It had been almost a year since he and Mossy Bell attended. After that one day Mama said they might as well stay home and work, if the big boys was going to kick dirt in their dinners. If Daddy was alive he could teach them to read the Bible for themselves. It was too far down to walk off the mountain anyway.

At only one place could Nelse see the children in the schoolyard. They were kicking a ball and chasing each other from end to end of the clearing. It looked as though James and Ulyss were pushing each other, and just as they were about to fight Carlton walked up and placed his finger between their faces. "Best man spits over my hand," he said. They both began spitting and hitting, but just then the teacher came to one of the doors and rang the bell. James and

Ulyss reluctantly followed the others back into the building, still shoving and trying to trip each other.

Crouching behind the brush Nelse watched the playground empty. The trees where he and Mossy Bell had sat down to eat were just in front of him. The pine needles were still pressed neatly by the winter rains, showing no sign of last year's kicking and scuffle.

It was only another mile to the Brevard road. Nelse dreaded the road because it was all muddy ruts, and there would be traffic on it. But it was the only way he knew to get to the store. People would ask him about the fawn as soon as they saw him.

He had no sooner reached the road, and was skipping along the shoulder trying to stay out of the cold puddles and thick-lipped ruts, when he met a mule and wagon. The driver had several sacks in the bed; he must be coming from the mill.

"Got yourself a pretty," the driver called. "Looks like he's anointed you already." And the man laughed as he creaked and lurched on.

Nelse had to walk on rocks across the creek, and then another wagon caught up with him.

"You want to ride, boy?" the driver called, slowing his two horses.

"No sir," Nelse said, and hurried on along the bank.

"You the Searcy boy from on the mountain?" the driver called as he passed. "The one that don't go to school."

"Yes sir."

"I knowed your pa," the man said.

"Yes sir." Nelse slowed down, hoping the wagon would go on.

"They's a doe probably looking for her little un," the man said. "But's a pretty little thing." He drove on past.

It must have been another two miles to the store. Nelse's feet were sore from the cold gritty mud.

HE HAD NOT BEEN to the store since Christmas when he brought a basket of eggs and half a pound of ginseng to trade for cloth and shoes. That's when Old Salem said there would be no more credit. The road was dry and dusty then, with dirt like soot on all the weeds and nearby bushes. The store sat on its pillars back from the creek, but now the water swirled right up to the platform of logs in front of the door. The spate from the rains made the creek look fast and dangerous. Horses were tied to the railing of the platform, and there were several wagon teams tethered to trees in the yard. A shiny salesman's buggy was tied to the post beside the pump. Nelse climbed the log steps into the dark store.

"Well look at this little feller," someone said. The speaker smelled of whiskey and wore a gray soldier's uniform ragged at the elbows. Nelse could not see much more in the dim light.

"Somebody robbed the cradle," another man said.

"You can't bring animals in here," the storekeeper said behind the counter. Old Salem looked bigger than Nelse remembered. He could feel the thimble in his pocket.

"But ain't he a pretty little thing," the man in the uniform said.

"Looks like he forgot hisself on you," the well-dressed salesman said.

The fawn, which had quieted down on the walk, was startled by all the talking. It trembled in his arms and wet him again.

"You're going to need to wash in the creek," the man in the uniform said.

"You'll have to get that thing out of here," Old Salem said. "I can't have it fouling my store."

"Aw, it's just wetting him. Ain't hurting a thing else," the salesman said. "Can I hold him?"

"He might jump," Nelse said.

"I'll hold him real good, boy," the salesman said.

"He'll wet your suit," someone said.

"Naw, I'll put a sack around him," the salesman said, picking up a feed sack. The salesman took the fawn in his large hands and held it out like a kitten or puppy. "Ain't he a cute bugger," he said.

Now that his eyes were adjusting to the dimness Nelse could see the men gathered along the counter and around the big pot-bellied stove. There was the driver who had passed him, and several men in boots and overalls, the loggers who had been cutting on the mountain and drove their logs down with the spring freshet. They must have got their money and were drinking some of it up in celebration.

"Your Maw got anything to pay on her account?" Old Salem said, leaning across the counter.

"She'll pay," Nelse said.

"What'll you take for this little thing?" the salesman said. "I'll bet my kids would love it."

"Hadn't thought to sell it," Nelse said.

"I'll give you a dollar for it, boy," the salesman said.

"Aw, he's an orphan boy," the man in the uniform said.

"Like as not he stole it hisself," the salesman said.

"He caught it and it's hissun," the man in the uniform said.

"I'll give you five dollars for him," the salesman said. "It's not worth it, but he's such a cute little thing."

Nelse was going to say yes, but one of the loggers lurched over to the salesman and said, "This here boy caught that deer all by hisself, which is more than any of you could do."

"Yeah," another said, "All by hisself."

"All right, make it seven," the salesman said. "Make it seven."

While the man in the uniform held the fawn wrapped in the sack the salesman counted out seven silver dollars into Nelse's hand.

"Now you can pay what your Maw owes," Old Salem said, "And have some left over besides."

"How much?"

"You'll have almost four dollars left."

"You treat him square, Salem," one of the loggers said.

Nelse stood at the counter as he had seen Mama do and ordered a bag of coffee beans, a bag of sugar, a dozen fishhooks, a poke of powder, a primer and speller for him and Mossy Bell, and a big piece of gingham cloth for Mama.

"That's all I can give you for the four," Old Salem said.

"I need a pocketknife," Nelse said.

"The four dollars is spended," Old Salem said.

"Give him a damn knife, you skinflint," one of the loggers said.

Old Salem handed him a Buck knife with two blades, and wrapped the other goods in brown paper, and tied string around the bundle.

"I'm buying a round all around," the salesman said, holding the fawn in the crook of his arm. There was cheering, and while the men were toasting the salesman Nelse slipped out the door with his package.

The sunlight blinded him for a moment, but the mud of the road was warmer now, and he noticed how the leaves were already out on the sycamores along the creek. It would be weeks before they saw leaves that big on the mountain that loomed blue in the distance above. The big trout would be in the headcreeks by now. He could feel the thimble still in his pocket. The package in his arms was light, even though he held it away from his still-damp shirt. He was careful to leave the trail before he got to the schoolhouse.

1916 *Flood*

IT HAD BEEN RAINING eleven days and nights. The ground was so saturated great chunks of mountainsides had broken away and slipped in mudslides down the slopes, knocking over trees and tearing out new boulders. The pasture hill ran with springs from several eyes in its soil. The fields, too wet to walk in, were festering with weeds. It was not time for laying the corn by yet, but the baulks had not been touched by a hoe or plow since the middle of June.

From where he lay Raleigh saw the river rising. First the current turned a dishwater tinge, as mud from the ditches and feeder branches began to cloud into the stream. Then the river grew reddish-brown and ugly in its spate, slapping overhanging branches, and tearing loose debris from the banks. Waves seemed to reach up and grasp at stumps, and pull everything underneath. The river moved faster, hurrying with the power of a freight train, accelerating between narrow banks. Its speed was hypnotic, as it inched up plucking away leaves and sticks, stirring saplings. From where he lay he watched the flood creep out of the banks, eating and lapping through the fringe of trees into the fields.

As it rained he lay with his cheek on the wet soil watching the river spread toward him. The brown water took the bottom land clod by clod and furrow by furrow, pulling at the watermelon vines along the lower edge and swirling into the corn rows. In the dark he saw the river widen out across the field as though spreading wings, pushing little sticks and lather along its edges.

Why had he thought it would not reach the cemetery? As the river spilled into the garden, floating gourds and squash, it washed into the hogpen and poured into the pit under the outhouse. The scouring backwash reached into the spring and dirtied the pool, and had almost reached the smokehouse where the meat lay on salty shelves.

Why had he not thought it would touch the graveyard? From where he lay, cheek on the wet dirt, he watched the water invade every trail in the pasture, find the playhouse under the pines, poke a cold finger in the snake holes under the crib. Only turf could resist the rub and pull of the current.

The new dirt on Mama's grave melted like sugar when the river reached the burial ground. From where he lay he was helpless to stop the advance, though he had to watch the destruction. The water came shoaling up the road through the woods, sweeping around turns, and pushing bird nests and hornet nests off brush.

At the end of the cemetery the front of the flood took jars of flowers, and toys off babies' graves. The red water approached mound by mound up the hill, as snakes and toads scurried before it. He cried out when the first water touched the raw soil on Mama's grave, but of course he could make no sound. The advancing water dissolved the mound and ate into the packed earth underneath.

From where he lay he watched the flood soak down and trickle through the new clods and shovelfuls of turf, sinking around pebbles and flowers thrown over the coffin. The water worked so fast it loosened all the tamped dirt around the pine box and spilled onto the casket itself. Daddy and Grandpa had ordered the rosewood coffin from town. It was the shiniest wood he had ever seen, polished and lacquered like a dark red mirror. But he refused to touch the box when it lay on two chairs in their parlor, and he refused to kiss Mama's powdered forehead as she lay in the front of the church, though Aunt Docie held him up to see her and said, "Kiss her one last time; it'll mean a lot to her in heaven."

From where he lay he wanted to cry that he would kiss her if he had the chance again, though he was still scared. But of course he could say nothing.

As water sank into the grave and the clods softened, the sealed coffin became buoyant. It rose in the pine box and pressed against the lid. As water swirled and the hill was eaten away, the mud in the mound above turned to slush and then liquid. The casket knocked its way upward through the pebbles and mud, pushing from wall to wall in the grave. The coffin tilted, and shivered within its container like a football held under water.

From where he lay he wanted to hold the coffin down, but it was too late. The flood had dissolved the soil above and there was nothing to stop its rise. Bumping on rocks, and the pine container, it pushed like a chick trying to break from its shell. A stone lodged on the lid held the box down for a moment longer, but the rocking motion rolled the weight to one side.

One end of the box rose faster than the other, perhaps because the feet were lighter than the head. As it reached the surface the box leaped clear of the water, and when it fell back the lid tore off the pine box, and the coffin slid into the waves. The impact loosened the latches, and the coffin lid swung open. And there was the rain beating down on Mama's face, melting the powder over the measles rash. The rain opened her eyes and she was looking at him.

WHEN RALEIGH WOKE, screaming silently, the rain was steady on the roof and in the gutter above his window. The tin roof hummed and the pipes swallowed as they had for weeks.

He did not know why he felt guilty about the rain. True, they had not been able to work in the fields that needed hoeing so badly. But there was nothing to do, while the rain continued, except sit in the crib and shuck the last of the corn. And he had gone fishing only once, on a day when it cleared up briefly, after the first five days of rain.

The pounding on the roof was ominous, and the drumming in the gutters. It was as though the world had been abandoned to flood as it was in the Bible. The sun was gone, and there was nothing but clouds and darkness and more rain. The hills were washing away, and the fields stood rotting in water.

If his dream was true, that the graveyard had been reached by the flood and the graves opened, he was somehow responsible. Mama had been dead for four years, but in his dream her grave was fresh as though she had been buried yesterday. Was that a sign she wasn't resting peacefully, because he had not kissed her, because he did not say his prayers? He shivered under the damp quilt.

"Get up," Missy was calling from the kitchen. He reached for his overalls, relieved the night was over, but dreading another long day of rain.

"Want to go to the homecoming at Poplar Springs?" Grandpa said as he laced his shoes in the kitchen.

"They won't have it because of the rain," Missy said.

"Maybe it will stop before dinner time," Grandpa said.

"I wouldn't go nowhere in the rain," Missy said.

"I figure it's time for it to stop," Grandpa said.

"It's never going to stop," Missy said.

"We're going to wash away like in the time of Noah," Raleigh said. "And I haven't seen no rainbows neither." But he hoped Grandpa was right. They took the milk buckets that Missy had been scalding. The handles were still hot and wet. Nothing would dry in this dampness.

Daddy was grinding coffee on the back porch. The freshly ground beans smelled especially good because nothing else seemed fresh or dry. The screen door had swollen so it no longer closed, and the varnish on the wood had melted to gum that stuck to his hand. The yard was mostly puddles, and while there was a raw earthworm smell, it was obscured by the scent of rot from the woods and barn. The rain had gone on so long everything was decaying. Mushrooms had pushed up through the grass like little snowmen, and raised through the duff under trees. Mold grew on bark and even green leaves looked blue and white with mildew. He and Grandpa splashed through the puddles as they ran to the barn.

Out of the corner of his eye he saw the water had now reached the edge of the chicken house. The bottom land was completely submerged, with corn rows standing in two or three feet of muddy backwaters.

"What will we do if there's no corn?" he said as they reached the hallway of the barn.

"We'll save some of it. You'll see."

The barn smelled stronger than ever. Water was seeping around the walls into the floor of the stalls. The manure and straw had turned into a stinking mush. They had not cleaned the stalls since the rain began.

Raleigh milked hurriedly. He wanted to get out of the barn and back to the house to wash his feet. Manure squeezed between his toes as he pulled at the teats.

After milking he and Grandpa turned the cows out to pasture. But instead of cropping the cows walked straight to the white pines and stood in their shelter. Only the horse seemed not to mind grazing in the rain. He stood right out in the downpour and cropped the tall grass, his tail free from swishing flies.

When they put the buckets of warm milk on the porch for Missy to strain Raleigh dashed back into the yard, and washed his feet in the biggest puddle.

"Hey, don't get the yard dirty," Missy called. "Go wash in the branch."

"The branch is in the field," he hollered back.

He washed his hands and wrists in another, cleaner puddle.

As he sat down at the table his hair was dripping and his overalls were wet. Missy made him place a towel on his chair. The oatmeal was hot and the biscuits just out of the oven.

"Let's have some sourwood honey," Grandpa said. "It's Sunday."

"Every day is just alike in the rain," Daddy said. "It must be a curse on the land. It's the year of the seventeen year locusts, and I ain't seen a one."

"It's the war in France," Missy said. She read the paper every day.

"The locusts have been kept in the ground by the rain," Grandpa said. "They'll come out when it stops. You can't stop them."

"The bridge at Saluda is washed out, and the bridge on the French Broad at Arden. Jarvis said a railroad tunnel collapsed, but I forget where," Daddy said.

"This may be the end of time," Missy said.

"No. The world will never flood again," Grandpa said. "That's a promise; that's what the rainbow is."

A clap of thunder broke in the sky straight above them, shaking the windows and rattling dishes on the shelves. There were echoes off the mountains, and then another clap, further away.

"That means the end of the rain," Grandpa said. "Let's go to the homecoming."

The graveyard was on the road to Poplar Springs. Raleigh would see if it was flooded. He would tell no one his dream.

BY THE TIME they were dressed for church the rain had stopped and the sun was out.

Raleigh polished his shoes and began to lace them up. But Grandpa said, "No use to wear your shoes. They'd be covered in mud in no time. You would ruin them."

Boys and girls always wore their new clothes, their best clothes, to homecomings. It was a way of showing off, where the most people would see. Missy carried her shoes as they walked up the road.

After eleven days of rain the grass in the pasture was a foot high and spotted with mushrooms. Weeds along the fences glittered with their load of drops. As the sun came out through thinning clouds the world seemed in shock, as though a light had been shown into a cave world of perpetual twilight. Everything was waking up again, blinking and stretching. The mountaintops were still covered with clouds, and strands of fog lifted out of the hollows, as steam rose off the river.

"Maybe there won't be a homecoming," Missy said, as she and Grandpa and Raleigh picked their way along the muddy tracks up by the spring.

"There's always a homecoming," Grandpa said. "Especially now that it's stopped raining."

"What if the bridge is out up by Garfield's?" Raleigh said.

"Then we'll take the footlog above the shoals."

"And what if the footlog is washed out?"

"There's another one further up at Bane's."

"Look there at Thunderhead," Missy said and pointed to the top of the mountain. As the fog cleared, the gash of a landslide was exposed.

"It tore away the cliff," Raleigh said.

"No, the cliff's further over."

"That big rock could have rolled down on top of us in the night," Missy said.

The big slide above them seemed to mean that the cemetery was certainly flooded, but Raleigh could not have explained the connection. He just felt sure the two events were related. Still, he wouldn't mention it. It was bad luck to talk about what worried you. Just talking could make it come true.

Above the spring, runoff from the pasture had filled the ditch with trash and then cut across the road, carving out a canyon through the ruts. The dirt here was golden and mealy, and flecked with mica. In the new sun the ground sparkled and signaled. The new gully was so deep they would have to fill it with rocks and brush before a wagon could easily cross.

On the roadbank every pebble stood on a column of dirt.

"How come it rained so long, Grandpa?" Missy asked.

"There's no telling about the weather," Grandpa said.

"Is it because of the war in Europe?" Raleigh said.

"There's no telling about the signs," Grandpa said.

"Sometimes we know how to interpret them, and sometimes we never learn."

"At least the spring's still clear," Missy said.

"It might have got some runoff and then cleared up again," Grandpa said. There was a ditch above the spring to divert water; its walls seemed intact.

Where their road connected with the county road another ditch had been washed. The erosion had undercut a white pine just at the gate and the tree had fallen across the entrance.

"We'll chop it away when we get home," Grandpa said.

"But we can't work on Sunday," Raleigh said.

"The Lord lets you get an ox out of the ditch on Sunday," Grandpa said. "I reckon this is a kind of ox in a ditch."

The whole family of the Brights were walking up the road. They were a big family from down near the cotton mill. Mrs. Bright carried a basket on her arm. Her husband carried only his walking stick.

"People ain't been living right," Mrs. Bright said. "And the Lord is sick and tired of it."

"Is the turnpike bridge intact?" Grandpa said.

"Still there, but I wouldn't cross on it," Mr. Bright said.

"The Lord has a way of reminding people of his power," Mrs. Bright said.

Raleigh fell in step with Grady Bright who was almost his age. They hadn't seen each other since the end of the school term.

"What you been doing?" Raleigh said.

"Catching frogs that come up out of the river."

"What for?"

"To make them jump back in the river."

"How come?"

"We burn their tails with a hot stick."

"And they come back out?"

"They have to escape the flood."

A great cut had been washed across the road at the forks to Poplar Springs. Several wagons had stopped at the lip of the gully. It would take a day of shoveling and dragpanning to fill in the wash. Raleigh and Grady stood at the rim which was still crumbling off into the rushing water. He could see the layers of dirt under the road, the top level packed with gravel, and underneath the sand of the earlier road, and then red clay beneath it all.

Someone has thrown a couple of fenceposts across the rushing ditch and they stepped singly across. The graveyard was just a little further up the road. Raleigh felt a pain in his knees as they approached.

"It's the locusts," Grandpa said.

"I don't hear nothing," Missy said.

"No, they're coming out. Listen."

But Raleigh was running on ahead. The sun was hotter now, and the mud was beginning to smell even more of rotted things, of sour roots, and decaying debris washed off the hill. The water-sickened weeds smelled as though they had been scorched and their leaves were starting to sour. He wondered if some of the stink could be coming from the graveyard above.

"Wait for me," Grady called.

But Raleigh did not slow down, and Grady ran to catch up with him.

"Hey, where you going?" Grady called.

Raleigh did not answer. He was getting too out of breath to talk.

The cows were out in Stacy's pasture cropping the wet grass. Raleigh could hear the suck and wheeze of their feet in the soft ground. When Mama died suddenly of the measles Raleigh was seven. It had been raining, and when Grandpa said she was dead he ran down the hill to the orchard and cried with his face against an apple tree, his tears smearing on the lichen soot of the bark. That tree smelled like the woods did today.

"I'm going fishing tomorrow," Grady said, as he caught up with him. "Nelse caught a seventeen-inch trout yesterday in the Johnson Hole with a grasshopper. The river's been washed out there something terrible."

The graveyard was just around the bend. Raleigh

climbed the bank and cut through the woods to get there quicker. His pants got wet on the undergrowth of sassafras and sweet gum.

"Where you going now?" Grady panted behind him. "We'll get wet."

They came to the edge of the burial clearing, and Raleigh expected to see it all under muddy water. But instead the hill was green and sparkling in the sun. Bees fizzed among the flowers on graves, and the juniper still stood by Mama's mound. The mound had been covered with grass for three years. The graves of the family, great-grandpa and Uncle Joe, and Grandma, stretched in a row across the crest of the rise.

Raleigh ran among the graves getting his feet soaked in the grass. He felt so light he could hardly keep his feet on the ground. He ran to the tulip poplar on the north side and shook a heavy branch so that drops showered on the grass, and he ran to the west side and climbed upon a boulder already warm in the sun.

"Hey, what's the matter?" Grady called.

But Raleigh only smiled and ran on.

When they got back to the road the others had caught up.

"Wish I had that kind of energy," Grandpa said.

"These younguns have the Lord's own joy to be back in the sunshine," Mrs. Bright said. She brushed a fly away from the cloth over her basket.

"They's whole towns washed away in Virginia," Mr. Bright said. "I heard it at the store yesterday. And the railroads can't run."

"The Lord has spared us," Mrs. Bright said.

The footlog over Cabin Creek was still intact, and they walked it one at a time. Water was backed up into the brush at both ends of the footlog, and the ford was buried under four or five feet of flood. The water shone like a polished floor under the trees. It was Missy who looked through a gap in the sweetshrub bushes and gasped. Raleigh thought she must have seen a snake in the limbs.

"What is it?" Grandpa said.

All crowded to the edge of the water where sticks and

bits of bark and bugs were floating. Small waves lapped at their feet. Raleigh saw a body in a gray coat lodged against a river birch. The face was turned away. Grandpa and Mr. Bright began wading out toward it, carrying sticks as though they expected trouble.

They rolled the body over in the muddy water.

"It's nobody I know," Mr. Bright said.

"The Lord help us," Mrs. Bright said.

"Raleigh," Grandpa called. "You run on up to Poplar Springs and tell them to bring a wagon down."

"I'll go with you," Grady said.

But Raleigh was already running. His feet blurred on the path and then on the road again. He couldn't hear Grady running behind him for the wind in his ears. He could not remember when he had felt such a thrill of speed. His feet seemed to be moving a foot above the ground.

For the first time he heard the locusts in the woods. They were all around him, chanting "pharaoh, pharaoh," as Grandpa said they would, remembering the plague in Egypt. The road ahead was muddy and scattered with puddles, and he jumped over some and skirted others. In the worst places he ran through the weeds on the shoulder. The stench of the flood was in his nostrils, but he felt as if he could outrun it. Though his assignment was solemn and serious, he felt he could outrun all troubles and fears.

Crossties

SCOTT CROSSED the Florida line just at sunrise. Russ and Dave were still asleep in the cab beside him and did not see the first orange light spread over the tops of the pines and gray fields. The sun seemed to come right up out of the earth. The highway ahead was paved with red gold, but it was built up on a kind of causeway which kept everything on the right except the telephone lines and the tips of the pines in shadow. As far as he could see the road ran straight until it pierced the red sky, and the telephone wires ran beside it, the three-tiered crosses merging far ahead in the glow. Sailor's warning.

Or maybe it was a good omen, a welcoming, after the all-day and all-night drive from the mountains. Without checking the map he knew they were less than a hundred miles from Daytona and the hotel construction sites. Russ had better be right about the hiring. All together they didn't have money for gas to get back home.

"They're rebuilding Florida after the Bust," Russ said. He had heard it in Asheville. The hotels and rooming houses were going up. The New York money was investing there again.

If they were approaching prosperous country it wasn't obvious yet, except for the gilding of the early light. He had seen nothing but shacks along some river, and old houses set among pines at the edge of fields. The oaks had the long weeping moss on them, and there were little palm trees along the telephone poles. But everything seemed either swamp or pine woods, with dirt roads wandering off and disappearing into the barrens.

Drowsy from the long night of driving, Scott hardly noticed the black pickup approaching from the side road. It was a Model T with several children standing in the bed. With nothing but open highway, complete visibility, there seemed no reason to slow down. In fact it seemed the Model T had stopped, or at least paused, and he was almost at it when he realized the driver was coming out into the highway.

He stamped his brake and heard the screaming of children in the other truck and saw the terror of the driver as he crashed into him. All in one instant Scott's face hit the steering wheel and Russ and Dave rolled onto the dashboard and the children in the other truck were screaming.

WHEN HE WOKE it was the smell of steam he noticed first. Russ was outside and pulling at him, and he breathed in the rust and rubber smell of a hissing radiator.

"Scott are you awake? Scott get out before it goes."

His face was stuck to the steering wheel, but he pulled away, his nose and cheeks hot and sore. Russ led him along the highway where cars were stopping and drivers gathering.

There seemed to be smoke drifting over all, but it was the steam from the radiator.

"We've got to get the driver out," someone yelled.

"Does anyone have a blanket?"

Russ led him over to the grass on the shoulder where Dave sat wiping the blood from his forehead. He seemed to be just waking up.

"Dadblast it, my head's bleeding," he said.

"It's just a cut where you hit the windshield," Russ said.

"What did you *do*? What happened?" Dave asked Scott.

Scott noticed the blood on his hands. It was dripping from his face. The blood came from his nose and mouth. He must have broken a tooth. His nose and cheek were sore, but nothing there seemed broken.

"We'll get the driver out," someone hollered again.

Scott wiped his hands on his pants and started toward the other truck.

"Don't go over there," Russ said. "You're in no shape to help."

"I'll go where I please," Scott said.

Blood from his nose dripped on the grass, and he saw the grass had stickers on it. The dirt of the highway shoulder was gray sand.

For the first time he saw the woman holding the baby, standing beside the road. She clutched the baby and looked at the grass. He had to get around her to reach the other truck. She had blood on the front of her dress and her left arm was red and blistered.

"You killed him," she said in a low hoarse voice, and looked at him. "This early morning you killed him."

The baby had blood in its hair, but it was the blueness of its skin he noticed. The baby was not crying, and its neck and cheek were blue. The woman held the infant closer to her chin and cried.

"Here, help. Easy now. Easy now."

They were dragging the driver from the Model T and Scott felt the overwhelming stench of radiator water. The man's face was only slightly bloody. His skin was white and peeling in little strips, like where a hog had been scalded.

A trooper in uniform pushed his way through the crowd. "Stand back everybody. Lay him on the ground."

The trooper bent down and listened to the bib of the wet and bloody overalls. Then he straddled the body and began to push down on the chest, pushing and then waiting, pushing again.

"Stand back," he said as the crowd edged closer.

Scott watched the white scalded face, waiting for a twitch or blink, a sign of breath.

"He was just drowned in the radiator water," someone said.

"More likely his lungs were seared with the steam," the trooper said. He pushed again and waited.

"He's scalded with the water and his chest is crushed."

The trooper pushed on the ribs again, and looked around. "Who's the other driver?" he said. Several pointed to Scott.

"He drove out in front of me," Scott said.

"Who else was in the truck?"

The dazed children who had been in the back of the Model T were pointed out where they stood or sat in the grass. And the crowd moved back so the trooper could see the woman with the baby.

"Ma'am, I'm afraid this man is dead," he said. The woman did not look up or answer. There were crows making a fuss in the pines nearby.

"He done it," one of the boys said, and pointed to Scott.

"Were you responsible?" the trooper said.

Scott shook his head, and wiped his nose on his sleeve.

"Who was with you?" the trooper said. Russ and Dave stepped forward. "Soon as the ambulance comes you all can come with me."

Scott felt the pressure of the eyes of all the crowd fastened on him.

"WE NEED TO GET our toolboxes," Russ said to the trooper as he motioned them toward the van.

"They'll be taken care of, along with the truck."

"Our tools are all we have," Scott said.

"They may be seized for damages."

"The collison was not my fault," Scott said.

"Tell that to the widow," the trooper said.

But he let them get their toolboxes from the pickup bed and then locked them in the black and white van.

The sun was up now, but there were no windows in the van except at the back. Through the wire mesh in front they could see the driver and glimpse the town they were driving into.

"Hey, where are we? What town is this?" Dave called to the driver. The cut on his forehead had bled down his cheek. He wiped his lips and called again, "What town is this?"

The driver did not answer.

"Ain't we in a pickle," Russ said, and began to cry. Russ had always been the weak one when it came to trouble.

The van smelled of rancid oil, and the sick from some drunk throwing up and only partly cleaned with lysol. Scott held the toolbox between his legs and tried to smell the machine oil on the saw blade and the hinges of the bevel. The tools were just odds and ends he'd collected over the years, a level bought in Columbia when he'd built barracks there during the war, a hammer that belonged to their Daddy on the mountain, the saw found in the cellar of a house they had rebuilt around the lake. There was a dent in the T-square where it dropped off a scaffolding in Asheville and hit a cement block. He had meant to get another one, and then after the Crash and Depression hit he was lucky to have any job. The hatchet he had bought as a boy when he got his first job helping to cut the right of way around the lake.

They crossed the railroad tracks before coming into town, the Coast Line they had driven beside in Georgia.

"We'll never get out of this place," Russ said.

"We'll just have to see," Scott said.

"A man starts out looking for work . . ." Dave said, but didn't finish the sentence. They drove around a small courthouse of yellow brick and turned into an alley. The building in the rear had bars on the windows.

"You can't lock us up without charging us," Scott said to the man behind the station desk.

"I can hold you on suspicion," the policeman said.

"Suspicion of what?"

"Criminal negligence, reckless endangerment, for a start."

"I was the only one driving," Scott said. "You can't lock them up, too. They were asleep when it happened."

"And for vagrancy. You all don't have three dollars between you."

"We could sell the tools," Russ said, "Just take us to a pawnshop."

The officer shook his head. He looked at each of them hard with his shiny brown eyes. "We've had a lot of agitators coming through here," he said. "For all I know you boys may be union agitators, communists, coming to stir up the workers just as the citrus crop comes in. We've been warned they are coming down from the North."

Scott felt the sweat stinging the cut in his lip. "We ain't nothing but carpenters looking for work," he said. "We can prove it. Look at my license."

"Agitators have perfectly legitimate credentials," the police chief said, coming out of his office in the back. He looked at Scott's license. "You boys from North Carolina?" he said.

"Henderson and Buncombe Counties."

"You don't have any moonshine in that truck do you?"

"No sir."

"None of that mountain corn liquor headed for Miami?" He looked close at Scott. "Lock them up," he said.

"Don't we get to speak to a lawyer?" Dave said. He was beginning to wake up from his daze.

"Can you afford a lawyer?" the chief said.

"Don't we get to make a phone call?" Scott said. "Our families can raise the money."

"In good time," the chief said.

Who would they call if they had the chance? There were no phones on the creek except at the store. Even Dave's family in Asheville didn't have a telephone. It would have to be a telegram. The policeman unlocked a door at the side and led them down a hallway of cells. They followed with their toolboxes, and he unlocked a cell and directed them inside.

There was a black man prone on the floor of the cell and a puddle of vomit near his head.

"Don't bother Willie," the officer said, "And he won't bother you." He locked the door and left them.

There were three cots in the room, and a black-haired

man with a week's growth of beard sat on one of them smoking.

"*Bon giorno,*" he said and laughed, exhaling smoke. "Put
down your luggage, gentlemen, and make yourselves at
home. Welcome to the best that Florida has to offer."

Russ sat down on one of the cots and began weeping
again. Scott put his toolbox down and looked at Dave.
"We've got to think," he said. Dave had worked for the road
department of Buncombe County in the boom time of the
twenties. He knew more about law and local politics than
Scott did.

"What are they going to do?" Scott said. "You can't arrest
somebody for being in a wreck."

"It may be local politics," Dave said. "There may be an
election coming up and a local scare about outside organizers."

The black-haired man on the bunk exhaled smoke and
chuckled.

"You know something about this?"

"Gentlemen, I don't know nothing," he said and spread
his arms.

"Or it could be they want to get money out of us, a bribe
or damages. A fine. Whatever they want to call it."

"Now they know we don't have nothing."

"They might hold us until we can get some from home."

"Welcome to the sunshine state," the black-haired man
said.

Scott sat down on his toolbox. His head ached and he
was sweating more than ever. Russ had lain down and
turned his face to the wall. Dave sat down on the other cot.
The man on the floor groaned in his sleep.

There was no one at home with any money except his
daughter Anna who made nine dollars a week at the dime
store in town. And part of that she paid to the boarding
house where she lived. Mary might have a dollar or two from
selling eggs at the store on the highway. The truck was the
only thing he had to sell, and it was not paid for yet. It was
probably worth nothing now, except as junk, and he still

owed for it and was behind on mortgage payments for the land. And the well-driller had not been paid since April.

Every cent made in the twenties had gone for the mortgage he and Russ had arranged between them. That was during the war when Russ was working in Detroit. But when the munitions work ended, he returned to the creek and married and spent all his savings on his own house. In the summer they farmed the cleared land, and in the winter worked at carpentry to pay off the mortgage. When there was no work, they cleared the swampy acres by the river, sawing down the maples and poplars and burning the trash. Once they burned a poison ash without knowing it, until the rash came out and blisters appeared everywhere on his face and arms where the smoke had touched. And they had to ditch out the bottom where the spring came out of the hill. The cost of the steam shovel was another debt.

But it was the typhoid epidemic that hurt. He was sick himself for a couple of weeks and couldn't work. But the fever hit his oldest son Billy hardest. For six weeks Billy lay unconscious with fever, raving in delirium, and every day they expected him to die. Twice the nurse wakened him in the night and told him to come quickly, it was the end. And after the crisis, when no one in the house could speak for fear it might disturb the boy, Billy was too weak to sit up for another month. When it was over and Billy was walking again he owed the doctor four hundred dollars. The county condemned his spring and ordered him to dig a well.

There was shouting outside the jail. It sounded like a parade or a meeting.

"What kind of holiday is this?" Dave said.

"It's no holiday. This is a week before Thanksgiving."

Scott climbed up on the end of the cot to look through the window, but the glass had been painted over with gray paint.

"It may be some kind of local celebration," he said.

"Any day's a good day for a lynching," the black-haired man said.

"What do you mean?"

"What's he done?" Dave said, pointing to the man on the floor.

"Oh it's not him; he's just drunk."

"What are you in here for?"

The man lit another cigarette, inhaled, and held his cigarette out as though inspecting it. "It's not even me they are mad about. At least I haven't killed anybody."

Russ sat up on the cot where it appeared he was sleeping. "We should have stayed on the place and hewed crossties," he said. "I knew we should not have left."

"It was you that insisted on coming to Florida," Dave said.

"Don't blame me. Scott was the one driving. He killed the man."

Scott climbed up on the cot again and listened at the cloudy window. There were many voices and shouts, but he couldn't make out a single word.

"You got us into this," Russ said. "We could be up on the hill above the pasture hewing crossties."

THE CHESTNUTS on the ridge above the pasture were all dead now. The blight had finally reached the stand in 1924. First they turned yellow in midsummer, and the next year they were bare. Now they had shed their bark and stood like bleaching skeletons, though the wood was still hard. In fact the wood seemed to harden with age. They could be sawed down and hewed by ax into crossties. The railroad would pay fifty cents, sometimes seventy-five and even a dollar for a real good tie, but it took most of a day to hack one out. But it was the only thing on the place you could sell in winter, except chickens and eggs and butter. A week's work hauled to the depot might bring three or four dollars. How many days he had stood on the hillside chipping with the ax, smoothing the sides of the beam, keeping the corners straight and sharp in spite of the grain. His hands got so numb he could hardly loosen the fingers from the handle. On cold days and rainy days he had stood there in the leaves knocking chips and shavings from the iron hard wood. The ginseng was mostly gone, except for the remotest coves beyond the Flat Woods, and it could only be dug when there were leaves and berries to recognize. The tan bark was now worthless, even if chestnut oaks could still be found, because they had chemicals to tan leather and didn't need the acid from bark.

The policeman who locked them in the cell walked down the corridor.

"When do I get to telephone?" Scott said.

"Here's a visitor for you," the policeman said, and motioned for the man behind him to come forward. He was young and slender, almost a boy, and carried a clipboard under his arm.

"Hello, I'm Ted James," he said, and shook hands through the bars. "Could I talk to you all for a little bit?"

"Are you a lawyer?" Scott said.

"No, I'm a reporter."

"A what?"

"A reporter, for the Jacksonville *Democrat.*"

Scott looked at the man on the other side of the bars readying his pencil over the clipboard. Then he looked at Dave and Russ and the black-haired man on the cot.

"What do you want?"

"I might be able to help you," the reporter said.

"How?"

"Tell your side of the accident. There are a lot of angry people outside, kinfolks and neighbors of McCarron."

"Of who?"

"Of McCarron, the man you killed."

"I didn't kill him. He pulled out in front of me."

"The police are saying you swerved out of your way to hit him."

"That's a lie. His kids and wife were there. They saw it."

"They corroborate the police evidence."

"I wasn't even driving. I was asleep," Russ said, moving close to the bars.

The man on the floor groaned, and the reporter seemed to notice him for the first time.

"Is he with you?"

"He's just a drunk who was here when we came," Dave said. "Say, buddy, do you think you can help us?"

"I might be able to." The reporter was writing on his board.

"We're just down here looking for work," Dave said. "See our toolboxes here."

The black man groaned again, and Scott thought the puddle by his head had grown larger.

"What kind of work are you looking for?" The reporter continued to write, even when no one was talking.

"Russ heard they were building hotels in Daytona. We're carpenters, as you can see from the tools."

"And you're not going to the citrus groves?"

"No, we're looking for construction."

"Maybe your tools are just a cover, you know, an alibi?"

"Let's not talk to him anymore," Russ said.

"You jackasses," the black-haired man said. "All of you are jackasses."

"We could be hewing crossties right now," Russ said.

"Were you asleep when you hit Mr. McCarron's truck?" the reporter asked.

"No, he ran in front of me like he didn't even look or he was blind. I hit him on the side; that proves he ran in front of me."

"So you're all brothers?" the reporter said. "Scott, Dave, and Russ, in the order of age?"

"No, Dave is the oldest," Scott said.

"So where are you from, up North, right?"

"North Carolina, Henderson County."

"What do you do there?"

"I'm a farmer. Russ and I are farmers."

"I thought you said you are carpenters."

"We are, part time, to pay for the mortgage."

"And where does he live?" he said, pointing to Dave.

"I live in Asheville. I'm a carpenter."

"Any final statement you would like to make?" the reporter said to Scott.

"I just want to say it was an accident and I'm sorry McCarron was killed. I have a family myself and I know how hard it will be for his widow and kids. It was not my fault."

"Was it his fault?"

"Yes it was."

"Thank you gentlemen." The reporter put his clipboard under his arm and left.

"Maybe he will help us get out," Russ said, sitting down again.

"In a pig's eye," the black-haired man said, and laughed.

"You laugh a lot," Dave said. "What is your game?"

"Oh nothing. Nothing at all."

"You keep acting like you know something."

"I don't know nothing, nothing at all."

"STAND BACK," the jailor called. He unlocked the door and set a tray on the floor. On the tray were four bowls of pinto beans, four squares of cornbread, and five cups of coffee. "The extra coffee is for him when he wakes up," he said, pointing to the man on the floor.

"When do we see a lawyer?" Scott said.

The jailor locked the door behind him. "You hear those people outside?" he said. "They'll see you anytime you want."

"You've got to charge us to hold us," Dave said.

The jailor looked at him and grinned. "Enjoy your lunch," he said.

AFTER EATING the pinto beans and drinking the tin cup of coffee, Scott sat down on the cot that was free. The weariness came over him at once. It felt as though a drug had been introduced into his blood. His arms felt so heavy he did not want to lift them, yet there was a lightness throughout his veins and nerves, as though each cell was floating separately, each molecule drifting into sleep. He had not slept all last night, and he had worried on his feet all day.

Instead of lying down on the cot, he leaned back against the wall and replayed the wreck in his mind. The Model T appeared in front of him and the driver looked in surprise as the geyser from the radiator sprayed over his face. Had McCarron screamed when he was burned? Was it his cry he had heard when he woke on the steering wheel, along with that of the children? He could not remember. Maybe Mc-Carron had died instantly as the steam seared his lungs. As they pulled him from the cab his face was peeling in white strips, but he was still alive, perhaps, his eyes open and looking at Scott.

The guard walked down the hall leading McCarron whose face was bandaged so he looked like a snowman or a mushroom. Only one eye was uncovered and visible through the gauze.

"Look who I brung to see you," the guard said.

The guard unlocked the door and McCarron entered the cell. His arm was in a sling, and under his overalls his whole body was bandaged.

"I just want you fellows to know I don't blame you for what happened," he said through the gauze.

"Tell that to the judge," the guard said.

"You're working fellows like me," McCarron said.

"Tell them we just want to go back home," Dave said.

"We'd be much obliged," Russ said.

The man with the black hair was laughing as though somebody had just said something extremely funny.

Scott stood up to shake McCarron's hand.

"Just to show you no hard feelings," McCarron said, "I'll show you this." He began to unwrap the bandages from his head, being careful not to tear any strips. As he unwound the white ribbons Scott saw his skin was white and tender as a grub worm's, and full of pus, and worms were wriggling through his forehead and out of his eye sockets.

WHEN SCOTT WOKE UP, the man with the black hair was laughing, and the black man on the floor was stumbling to his feet. The jailor stood at the door. He had just said, "Time to get up Willie. Time to get up and go home."

As the man got on his feet his eyes met Scott's for a moment, as if to pass a message. But Scott did not know what it could mean. He did not seem to have the look of someone hungover and sick. The black man shuffled out, and the jailor locked the door again.

"Hey, when do I get my paper?" the black-haired man yelled. "I paid to get the paper."

"You'll get it when I'm ready to bring it," the jailor said.

The tray and cups and bowls were gone. Scott did not know how long he had been asleep, but the light through the dirty window was different. There were voices in the street outside, but lower than before. Russ was asleep on the other cot.

The puddle of vomit was drying in the center of the floor.

"At least we're rid of him," Dave said.

"That's their pigeon," the black-haired man said.

"You mean he wasn't drunk."

"Oh, he'd had a few drinks, to seem credible, but he's been in three times since I've been here. The other two times he talked to me. He's their ears."

"Why him?"

"What better cover. He's black, and supposedly an arrested drunk. Who would ever guess it?"

"But the puke?"

"Yeah, the puke. I don't know how he does it. Maybe he sticks his finger down his throat. Maybe he has a little bag of colored cream of wheat in his coat to squeeze out."

"What do they want to know?" Dave said. He sounded sleepy, befuddled.

"They want to know if you're outside agitators, dummy." The black-haired man lit another cigarette. "The orange season is about to start, and the big growers have ordered the police to keep all union organizers out of north Florida. A strike could bring them to their knees in a week or two, with fruit rotting on the trees."

"Are you an organizer?" Dave said.

"Maybe I am and maybe I ain't." The black-haired man blew smoke into the middle of the cell. When he talked he did not look at anyone.

The voices outside had gotten louder again. For the first time Scott could make out the word "murder" in the roar, and "Communist bastards."

"We're in trouble, friends," the black-haired man said.

THE JAILOR WALKED UP to the bars and threw a newspaper through to the black-haired man. "See if this will cheer you up," he said, and returned down the corridor.

The black-haired man scanned the headlines and front page. "It just don't look good," he said, and handed the paper to Scott.

"Three From Up North Kill Local Farmer," the headline read.

Under the byline of Ted James the story began, "Three men from North Carolina, suspected by the Volusia County police of being labor organizers, collided with a local truck this morning on Highway One, and killed the driver, Wilky McCarron, and his daughter Venice, aged one. The three are being held in the county jail awaiting arraignment."

"But when I told him our story he seemed to believe me," Scott said.

"Reporters have their orders," the black-haired man said.

"This is a godless place," Dave said. "We've got to pray."

"A lot of good that will do," the black-haired man said.

Scott stumbled on his toolbox as he walked across the cell and back. The voices outside were quieter for a moment. Someone was making a speech, and then there was cheering.

"We'll ask them to move us to another town, after dark," Scott said.

"They have to charge us first," Dave said.

"They can't hold us but twenty-four hours on suspicion," Russ said, sitting up. "After that it's *habeas corpus.*"

"Don't count on it," the black-haired man said.

Scott sat down on the cot. He had to calm himself. The worry had made him feel drunk, as though he was leaning inside himself, out of control. Who could he call in North Carolina? Lum would still be at the store. He could ask him to call a lawyer in town, or call the government in Raleigh, or the FBI. Someone had to know they were being held without being charged.

But if he called Lum he would have to tell Mary and Russ's family. They wouldn't know what to think, and they wouldn't know how to find out more. He would have to wait.

Except for the mob outside it only made sense to wait. Even if they would let him make a call, which they hadn't.

People would be stopping at the store now on their way home from the cotton mill. Everyone would find out he was in jail, if he called Lum. The kids would be home from school, and the boys would be out chopping wood before they did the feeding and Mary the milking. Or instead they would have taken their boards out to the pines on the pasture hill and be sliding down under the trees on the glistening pine needles. They would be lucky if they didn't cut their throats on the wire fence below. They wouldn't get back to do the feeding until dark, leaving Mary to chop the wood.

Mary, likely as not, was sitting by the fire talking to that silly Rosie who had just come by. They would have a cup of coffee before it was time for her to leave. And then Mary would start stirring things in the kitchen, boiling water for potatoes, before she rushed out to the barn, in the last of the sun.

When the jailor brought the bowls of beans for supper, Dave stepped up to the door. "You can't hold us without charging us," he said.

"Step back from that door or I'll take it away."

"We have the right to make a phone call," Scott said.

"Not until you're charged."

"Then I demand you charge us or let us go."

The jailor set the tray on the floor and backed away. "You boys are in no shape to demand anything," he said. "If we let you go those folks out there would tear you to pieces. They're neighbors and friends of McCarron, and they'd love to have a talk with you."

"You have twelve more hours to charge us or let us go," Dave said, but he sounded tentative, as though he no longer believed he seemed business-like, a former official of Buncombe County.

"When I come back everybody can go piss," the jailor said and left.

"I DON'T WANT any more fart food," Russ said when Scott handed him the bowl.

"Suit yourself."

"All my life you've got me in trouble and told me what to do. We get out of here I'm through with you."

"Big brave Russ. I've been cleaning up your mess since you were a baby."

Russ threw the bowl of beans at him, and the juice went over his shirt and pants. Beans were stuck to his clothes and scattered all over the cell and cot.

"Big brave Russ."

They circled each other around the puddle of vomit. The black-haired man was laughing again.

"What are you whinnying at?"

"Oh nothing, sport."

"Then you are a fool."

Scott stopped directly in front of the black-haired man and looked hard into his face.

"You don't think it's funny," the man said. "I'm stuck here with you hillbillies while the peckerwoods gather outside to lynch us, and the fruit hangs in the trees all over Florida while half the country is starving, and all you hicks can do is throw beans on each other."

Scott sat down on the cot and began picking the beans off his shirt and pants. He started to flick them onto the floor, but instead ate them, one at a time, keeping his eyes on the black-haired man.

"Maybe you are some kind of pigeon too," he said.

The man laughed again. He put his bowl down on the floor and lit another cigarette, and chuckled to himself while he smoked.

The shouts outside were louder, and there was cheering. Something banged against the wall, shattering like a soft drink bottle. A door opened down the hall, and they could hear the noise more directly.

"If I ever get out of here I'm going to run you off the creek," Russ said to Scott. "I'm through with your running things."

"Shut up," Dave said. "We'll be lucky to survive the night. You two want to die quarreling? We're a long way from home."

Suddenly the noise outside stopped. There was somebody talking in the office down the hall. Everybody in the cell was still. As Scott listened he saw there were beans on the toolboxes, and somebody had stepped in the vomit while he and Russ were circling. He looked at his shoes in the dim light.

Russ started to speak, but Dave motioned for him to keep quiet. There were car doors slamming outside, and engines starting. A clock struck, but Scott lost count of the hours. In the argument he had broken open the cut on his lip, and he wiped it with his sleeve. Sweat stung in the wound.

They waited a long time. The only sounds were cars passing outside, and low voices in the office. It must have been near midnight when the jailor walked down the hall and unlocked the cell. "Get your stuff and come with me," he said.

The black-haired man stood up.

"Not you," he said. "Just them." He saw the beans scattered over the floor. "You have bad table manners," he said.

They carried their toolboxes down the corridor to the office. In the bright light by the desk they blinked for a few seconds. There was a woman with the police chief, and the state trooper who had arrested them.

"You all know Mrs. McCarron," the chief said.

It was indeed the woman from the wreck. She looked more washed out and tired than ever, but she had a clean dress on and she carried a handkerchief.

"Mrs. McCarron, you said the wreck was not nobody's fault," the chief said.

"I can't abide no injustice," the woman said, looking at the floor as she spoke.

"Are you willing to sign a statement that the wreck was an accident and withdraw charges?" the chief said.

"It was Wilky's fault. He never was no driver, and I reckon the sun was in his eyes. He just ran out in the road like a dumb chicken."

"Will you sign an affidavit?"

"I couldn't stand innocent men going to jail," she said.

"My baby's dead, and my man. But I don't want anybody to suffer wrong for it."

"Here, we've drawn up a statement for you to sign, Mrs. McCarron."

But she did not look at the paper. She kneaded the handkerchief and stared at the floor.

"My baby's dead but I don't want anybody else's suffering on my conscience. This morning my boys was just shocked and mad, and they blamed it on them fellers."

After she made her scratch on the paper the clerk held out, the jailor led her outside.

"Thank you ma'am," Scott called after her, but she did not look back.

"YOUR TRUCK can't be fixed," the chief said. "It's worth a few dollars in scrap, but I suggest you let us give the money to the McCarrons. I doubt they have enough to bury him and the little baby."

"That's fine," Scott said. "That's fine."

"How are we going to get back?" Russ said, but nobody paid any attention to him.

"There's one other thing," the chief said. "I want you to sign this for Mr. Wilson here." He pointed to the trooper.

"What is it?"

"Just a form that says you won't blame him for arresting you."

"I treated you square," the trooper said. "After all, the boys blamed you."

Scott set his toolbox down and took the pen.

"I wouldn't sign nothing," Russ said.

Scott signed and handed the paper back.

"You boys are free to stay the night here," the chief said. "Don't reckon you have a place to sleep."

"No, we'll move on," Dave said.

"Suit yourselves. Here's your money." The jailor emptied their two dollars and some change from an envelope onto the desk.

"Ain't got no moonshine in those boxes?" the chief said, and smiled.

WHEN THEY WALKED OUT into the cool night air Scott saw on the courthouse clock it was a little after two. Lugging their toolboxes they crossed the square to the railroad tracks. They could tell where the tracks were by the white X signs and the light of the semaphore. The surfaces of the rails shone in the starlight.

"Which way do we go, up or down?" Dave asked. They paused in the dark, the toolboxes heavy in their hands. Then all turned without comment north, and started walking on the crossties.

"They put them at just the wrong distance on purpose," Russ said.

"These may be ties you have hewed," Dave said.

They walked for a while, then rested the toolboxes on the track, until the rumble of a southbound train sent them sliding down the gravel bank and into the brush beside the roadbed. Scott felt how dead tired he was as the freight roared by, the elbows of the locomotive pumping. When the train was gone he just sat where he had dropped. The others were already asleep. Dawn found them still there, their heads propped on the toolboxes.

When Scott woke the sun was already gold on the palmettoes. He brushed the sand from his pants and stood up. Dave and Russ were still snoring in the weeds. The ends of the crossties on the bank above reminded him of how he would spend the winter, if he got to keep the place somehow. Right now Mary was out at the barn milking, and the boys shelling corn for the chickens. He heard a humming in the tracks.

War Story

"Now WATCH HER dance at her own wedding," Uncle Doug said, and made the furry Eskimo doll walk down the tilted zoo book.

"Ah, she's not dancing," Ellie said. She had played with the walking doll last night, after Uncle Doug came home with it in his duffel bag, and she knew how it walked because of the weights inside, and the legs on hinges. She knew dolls didn't have weddings either.

"You better have your last breakfast as a free man," Frances called.

It was quiet around the table. Grandpa Harm said they might get Troy's letter today. But Grandma said it didn't matter since half of what he wrote was blacked out anyway. All he could talk about was how much it rained in East Anglia.

"Where's Caroline?" Uncle Doug said.

"Still in the bedroom. A bride shouldn't be seen on her wedding day before the ceremony."

"I want to go, I want to go," Ellie yelled. Uncle Doug put his arm behind her chair and flicked her right ear. But she knew that trick by now. "Can I go?" she said.

NEITHER GRANDPA HARM nor Grandma came out on the porch to watch them get into Troy's old Dodge. Uncle Doug had some trouble at first starting it; the engine whined and quit, whined and quit, but finally roared out a blue fog from the tailpipe. Ellie and her mother sat in the back and Caroline, who had emerged from the bedroom in a white suit and hair falling in curls on her shoulders, slid in close to Uncle Doug.

"Where is this preacher anyway?" Caroline asked, feeling her hair as though searching for something.

"Just down in Saluda."

"Where?"

"Saluda, halfway down the mountain."

"Mama would die if she was here," Caroline said. She had a way of half-shrieking and half-laughing that Ellie found strange for a grownup.

"When I told Daddy I wasn't coming back to the cotton mill, he said, that means you're getting married. But I wouldn't answer. And Mama wouldn't even look at me when I left for the bus."

Ellie tickled the back of Uncle Doug's neck above his uniform, but Frances slapped her hand away. "Don't bother anybody that's driving."

Saluda was just one street between the mountain and the railroad track. They stopped in front of the fire department and a man came out from the rear buckling his belt. When he got into the back with her and Frances, Ellie noticed he had a scar over his eyebrow. "Praise the Lord, it's going to be a glorious day," he said.

"Can I sit up front?" Ellie begged.

"No, stay here on my lap."

"She can come up here," Caroline said. "We've got plenty of room." Ellie climbed over the seat and squeezed between them, the gear shift between her knees.

It was still early and almost nobody was out in Saluda. The filling station was closed and Douglas said he hoped they had enough gas to reach the Greenville highway.

"If we run out Ellie can push," he said.

"Papa gave me his rationbook," Frances said. "But he didn't want Mama to know."

"The Lord has just enough rationbooks for his own," the preacher said.

They turned west across the tracks and up a steep hill, past big summer houses and long black cars in driveways.

"Rich people must still have gas," Uncle Doug said.

The end of a busted watermelon sat like a cap on a mailbox and a beer bottle balanced on the tongue-like door.

"Soldiers on leave will do anything," Caroline said, and, looking at Uncle Doug, laughed.

They wound around the dusty road into the mountains.

"Where are we going?"

"We'll get married up on Caesar's Head where we can see four states." Uncle Doug leaned across Ellie to kiss Caroline and almost ran into a culvert.

The road was badly washed out and the car bucked on potholes and the bedrock exposed in the ruts.

"Why this is Dark Corner," Frances said, holding onto the strap.

"It's near Dark Corner, honey," the preacher said. "Nobody lives in Dark Corner."

"Still country," Uncle Doug said. "Maybe we should stop and get a pint." He looked at Caroline.

"I'll not marry no drinking man."

"Some of the best people I ever knew lived in Dark Corner," the preacher said. "You was saved at my revival here in '30, before I lost the tent, wasn't you Doug?"

"No, at Tracy Grove in '32."

"I want to get saved," Ellie said.

THEY STOPPED at a filling station made of slabs and rusting Orange Crush and Pepsi signs. It was closed.

"I bet there's somebody in there asleep," Caroline said, and reached across to hit the horn. The gas pumps stood like skinny robots, their dial-heads covered with dust. The toilets were out behind the drooping clothesline. No one came out.

"How far is it to the highway?"

"I prayed through on this this morning," the preacher said. "The Lord will get us there."

"We'll run out of gas, I know it," Caroline said. "If Mama could see me now she'd die."

When they started again the car jerked and hiccoughed, bucking. "See, it's tired," Uncle Doug said to Ellie. "It don't want to go."

"Ah, I see your foot doing that on the pedal," Ellie said.

THE ROAD FOLLOWED the creek into a narrow valley. Ragged cornpatches brimmed out of hollows, and beds of dying potato vines. They passed a house with several school buses on their axles in the yard.

"Let's stop and ask how far it is," Frances said. "Maybe they could sell us some gas."

Uncle Doug drove into the rocky yard and blew. A man in overalls with no shirt stepped out on the porch. He didn't have any gas but bet they could get some at his son's house, two miles down the road. The son kept gas for his tractor.

"But I got some pretty roas'n' ears for sale though."

"We could take some to Mama."

"No, she's got a row just coming in."

"Would you like some, preacher?"

They bought two dozen ears of corn and put them in the trunk.

There was nobody at the son's house, or at least nobody came out when they blew. Further on the road got rougher and narrower, crossing and recrossing the creek, sometimes on shaky log bridges, sometimes by fords where the car stalled momentarily in the current and went on. There seemed to be crows over every field, and around the cliffs on the surrounding ridges.

"If Mama knew where I was she'd up and die," Caroline said, wiping her eyes.

The preacher remembered he had forgotten his Bible.

Ellie turned and looked at him over the seat, and kept staring as the car banged and rattled on.

"Don't stare," Frances said.

"How old are you, honey?" the preacher asked.

"Three three three," she sang and turned to the front.

THEY CAME to another filling station, same as the first except several men sat out front on chairs and bottle crates. The young men were unshaven, with long sideburns. They wore leather jackets even though it was not cold. Two motorcycles with fringed and jeweled saddlebags leaned near the gas pumps. Both had lots of mirrors and gadgets on the handlebars.

When the car stopped nobody moved toward them. The men sat exactly as they were and stared. Uncle Doug hit the horn.

"What's wrong with them?" Caroline laughed. "I've got to go to the bathroom." She opened the door and hurried past some overturned cars to the red white and blue toilet.

One of the older men shuffled over to the Dodge. "Ain't got no gas," he said. "None for a month. Can't get rationing."

A younger man leaned on the car near Frances' window. Tobacco juice stained his mustache and beard. "I got two gallon I could sell for a dollar." His foot weighed on the running board. "A dollar a gallon." He brought a can from inside and poured its contents into the car. Uncle Doug handed him two ones.

When Caroline returned she was silent until they were several hundred yards up the road. "There was a baby doll, or a real baby, in that toilet," she said. "I couldn't tell which. Just dropped through the seat, not more than ten inches long with a twisted head."

"It was just a doll," Uncle Doug said, glancing at Ellie.

"Some little kid dropped it there," the preacher said.

They reached Greenville about eleven. Frances and Ellie waited in the car while Uncle Doug and Caroline went into the courthouse. They watched the electric buses tethered to overhead cables. Uncle Doug had given the preacher three dollars to buy a new Bible.

"Why did they go in the courthouse?" Ellie asked. She noticed it was connected to the jail.

"To get a license. In South Carolina you can get a license in a day."

As THEY WERE DRIVING out of town, past the army camp and then a small lake, Frances said, "That's where they caught the man trying to poison the water supply."

"Did they ever prove it on him?"

"He had a pound of strychnine in a bag."

"Why would anybody ever think of such a thing?"

"He must have been a German. He had cousins over there."

They saw a sign, *Come Up To Caesar's Head*.

"I always wanted to see Caesar's Head," Caroline said.

They stopped at a diner for hotdogs and dopes and drove on, back toward the mountains.

"I have to pee," Ellie said, after about twenty minutes. They stopped the car to let Frances take her off into the brush. Ellie got out ceremoniously, and marched ahead of her mother into the scrub pines. She had to stop two more times also.

"Aunt Ida says there's a crack in Caesar's Head you couldn't fit a knifeblade in when she was a girl, and now it's more than six inches. When that big rock breaks off the whole country will sink."

"Aunt Ida's been saying that since 1903."

The preacher was silent, holding his new red and black Bible. The countryside was orange with dust. They passed a sawmill where the air was thick with smoke from the kiln. Big weathered houses, with columns and turrets, looked down from hilltops. The watermelon fields were scattered with pink and drying flesh that looked like cotton candy. There seemed to be crows over every patch and pine tree.

"Is Caesar's Head right on the line?" the preacher asked. "For we have to stay in South Carolina since that's where the license was bought."

"We'll stay just a few feet over the line," Uncle Doug said, "Except for Ellie, she'll have to stand in North Carolina."

"I won't."

It was getting overcast and dark. The clouds were heaviest above the mountains where they were heading. They could see a tower on the summit and lightning falling all around it.

"It'll be pouring," Caroline said.

"I just hope it's not raining all the way to Asheville," Uncle Doug said.

"Where are you staying?" Frances asked. "Not that you need to tell."

"At Grove Park Inn." Uncle Doug looked at Caroline and grinned.

"That will cost way too much," Caroline said.

"Can I come too?"

"You'll go home and see Grandma," Frances said.

"It ain't fair." Ellie looked at her lap. Uncle Doug reached around behind and tickled her right ear, but she seemed not to notice. "I'll get you another dancing doll," he said.

The first big drops hit the dusty windshield just as they began to climb. It rained hard, as the windows clouded over and the engine chugged on the steep curves.

"Man who built this road hung himself because he couldn't fit another curve in," Uncle Doug said.

The thunder was close and doom-heavy. Uncle Doug said it reminded him of magnesium flares and bombs. And of the earthquakes in the Aleutians.

"I've seen that island turn all the way over," he said. "I was laying in my bunk and suddenly the clothes on the rack all stood out straight and just stayed there. One old boy just put his .45 in his mouth after that and pulled the trigger."

To keep Ellie from crying Uncle Doug let her play a game with the knob on the steering wheel. Every time it came around she had to touch the blue and white ball and return her hand to her lap before he could grab it. As he swung the car around the switchbacks and hairpins up the mountain, they kept slapping and jerking away, until Ellie began laughing and slapping at him, even when the knob didn't pass near.

"Be still," Frances said.

Just as they reached the summit the rain slackened.

"It looks like there's an opening in the clouds," Frances said. They stopped in the parking lot just as the rain quit. Ellie could see the tower still halfway in the clouds. Soon as the door was open she crawled over Caroline and ran toward the fence, but the man at the gate stopped her.

"You come back here," Frances called.

Uncle Doug paid for them all to go out on the rock.

"It's a little dangerous right now on the tower," the man said, "From the lightning. You could wait just a little bit." He looked at the preacher with his Bible.

"I've been waiting a whole year for this," Uncle Doug said, and put his arm around Caroline and walked to the top of the cliff.

"Where's the head?" Ellie asked as they followed.

"It's the shape of the rockface; it's down under us," Frances explained.

"I wish Mama could see this," Caroline said as they reached the highest part and looked down on the country they had crossed. Clouds of separate storms were still floating over the piedmont, but the main storm was breaking up. They could see the tiny roads and houses, and smoke from sawdust piles. The preacher positioned them on a flat spot, just as the sun cut through and made the whole dripping wilderness and pools on the rock glisten. There was a rainbow over the forests below.

"I want to stand with them," Ellie said.

Frances pulled her back. "You stay here with me."

"Dearly beloved," the preacher began, holding his Bible over his chest. Uncle Doug took the ring from a little box that opened like a hippopotamus mouth.

Caroline had tears when it was over. They kissed and walked out to the edge. Ellie followed them.

"Terry Creek where I was born is there," Uncle Doug said, pointing.

"I just wish Mama could see all this," Caroline said. Ellie came up behind them and yelled "Boo!", pushing Uncle Doug a little. The force was just enough so that, surprised, he lost his footing and stumbled on the wet rock, before regaining his balance. He pulled Caroline to him and laughed.

Frances screamed when she saw them slip and then stand up again. She ran straight to Ellie and jerked her back from the edge, digging her nails into the little girl's wrists. The preacher, still clutching his closed Bible, had been looking up at the tower, and heard only the crows circling the topmost platform. He did not notice that both women as well as Ellie were crying, or that the last lightning of the storm was reaching out a delicate wand to touch the mountaintop.

Let No Man

FOR THEIR HONEYMOON Josie chose the Carolina Winds at Myrtle Beach. She had never been to the beach but her cousin Willa had gone there on her honeymoon five years ago and talked about it ever since. Not only was there a view of the ocean from the suite, there were extras such as a vibra-bed, breakfast in bed sent up from the restaurant, and a bottle of champagne in ice when you arrived. She and Nathan would not have the champagne, of course, but Willa said you could ask them to substitute ginger ale. The suite was done in white and the faintest pink, with the curtains, counterpane, carpets, and bathroom set matching. There was a dressing table with make-up lights also.

"It costs a hundred twenty-five a night," she had told Nathan when they were planning the wedding.

"It better be worth it," he said and grinned.

Both the wedding and reception were bigger than they had dared count on at first. Josie had saved for almost fifteen years, since she graduated from high school and started at the cotton mill, and when she talked to the lady at Bridal Fashions she kept finding things to add to the ceremony, including matching dresses for her two nieces who would carry the train, a little tuxedo for Nathan's nephew who would carry the ring, a flower trellis for the altar, a photographer with an assistant to get every part of the ceremony and reception from different angles. They even talked about asking the young preacher from town who had conducted a successful revival at church last year, but Nathan said that would offend Preacher McCall.

Josie felt lucky they had ordered extra for the reception. She had rented the Convention Room of the Grand View Motel out on Highway Forty-Seven, and the restaurant there catered the refreshments. They had a special called Campaign Punch which was pink and tasted of cherries and pineapple. More than a hundred people came, including family on both sides and acquaintances from the office at the cotton mill. Even Nathan's foreman from the Abrams Construction Company was there. And Uncle Paul was sober, wearing a suit coat over his overalls. He might have had a drink—he put on extra aftershave to hide the smell—but he wasn't intoxicated.

Her mother had not cried, but Nathan's mother did. Surely she couldn't be sad to see her son leave home at the age of thirty-eight, Josie thought. They would be living no further away than the cotton mill village. Several people had brought their Instamatics to the reception, and between them and the two professional photographers there were flashes going off again and again. Josie took her glasses off once, but felt so lost she put them on again to see who she was talking to. The lenses swelled her eyes big and close in photographs, but there was nothing she could do about it. People congregated by age and family group at the tables. Nathan stood in a corner with his boss and some buddies, but Josie wished he would stand with her to greet people. A man will never come and go to please no woman, her mother had told her.

Willa motioned to her from the rear door of the convention room, and pointed first to her watch and then at Nathan. They had planned it so if they left by three they would get to Myrtle Beach by eight. It was time to go.

Willa had Nathan's car waiting behind the motel. "You have to leave quick now. No hugging and well-wishing and rice throwing, or you'll be after dark getting there," she had said. Josie waited just outside the door while Willa brought Nathan out blinking in the July sun.

Josie's little Chevy was newer than Nathan's Trans Am, but he wanted to take the bigger, faster car. "You need to have power for a long trip," he said.

She hugged Willa and gathered the dress about her to get into the car. No one apparently had seen them leave. When they started she thought at first the noise was the glass packs in the muffler, but by the time they had gone twenty feet it was obvious hundreds of cans had been tied to the rear bumper. By the time they reached the exit at the front of the building all the guests were out in the driveway, rice in their hands, and the windshield sang as the hard grains hailed down, many splashing through the windows.

"I wouldn't trust Willa nowhere," Nathan said as they merged onto the highway.

"She means well. She wants us to have big memories." Josie picked the rice off her dress and flicked it out the window, except for a few grains she slipped into her change purse as keepsakes.

"She promised to get us away quiet." He seemed angry, but Josie couldn't help laughing as they rattled and hummed along. People in other cars and in yards by the highway were all looking at them.

They stopped at the rest area past the state line to cut the strings from the bumper. "Just Married" had been scrawled in white paint on the trunk. Nathan tried to rub it off with his hand, but it was real housepaint. His thick calloused hands looked especially rough in the French cuffs. Josie had rented the tux for him, but only at the last minute had he agreed to wear it. Some of the cans had been wired underneath, and he had to take off his coat and lie down to undo them.

THE FURTHER INTO SOUTH CAROLINA they got the hotter it was. The Trans Am did not have air conditioning and it seemed to give off extra heat under the dashboard. "That's because the engine is so powerful," Nathan said. "It runs hot summer and winter."

Josie had to take off her glasses again and again to wipe away the sweat. The cornfields of the piedmont were blasted by summer drought. Even the trees seemed wilted by the heat, the leaves flapping white in the breeze. The road shimmered and rippled ahead into the pollution-purple haze. Riverbeds were just bleached rocks with a wet thread through the middle. For fifty miles after Spartanburg they passed one factory or mill after another. The shopping malls looked like great palaces surrounded by a cobble of cars. At a distance the parking lots seemed full of M&M's, she thought. At a high school a football team practiced in shorts. The haze glowed over everything.

Once they reached the flat country the towns got smaller and older. They were off the expressway now and driving right through the middle of every town, along the railroad tracks and around Confederate monuments.

"It's a hundred miles closer to the beach in South Carolina," Nathan said.

"You said that before, but I don't see how."

"Look here at the map. The coast swings in in South Carolina. The ocean is almost south of the mountains."

They were in the town of Pageland ("Watermelon Capital of the World" the sign said) when she began noticing the funny smell. It was like the scent of a garden hose in the sun, and the hot water on the gasket of the pressure cooker.

"What is that stink?" she said. "This car's not burning up I hope."

"It always runs hot."

Tiny droplets began hitting the windshield.

"I didn't think it was raining," she said. "That looks like a drizzle."

The droplets didn't dry up on the glass, but stuck like syrup or specks of green honey.

"Must be honeydew," Nathan said.

"This ain't the honeydew time of year."

When they stopped at a red light steam rose from around the hood and there was a churning sound inside.

"The Lord gosh," Josie said, "This thing's burning up."

Nathan pulled into the first gas station they came to. By

then the car was smoking and jerking, and grunts and moans came from the radiator. When the attendant raised the hood and opened the cap steam shot all around, and the man backed away holding the cap in his rag.

"You've been running hot," he said. "It's the thermostat closed. Hear that thing chugging down there, as the steam tries to get through."

"Can you put one in?" Josie asked. She could feel the sweat thickening on her skin. The back of her dress was soaked and there was sweat in her bra and at the waist of her dress. She should have changed back at the Grand View.

"It's almost closing time," the man said.

"We're supposed to be in Myrtle Beach by eight."

"'Fraid you won't make it," the attendant said. "I'd like to help you folks out but the parts store just closed half an hour ago."

Josie took a Kleenex out of her purse and wiped her glasses. The mascara had run around her eyes and she cleaned the lashes as carefully as she could.

"Things close up here at five thirty on Saturday." The garageman looked at the "Just Married" on the trunk and shook his head.

"We'd be much obliged if you could help us," Nathan said.

"I could if I had a thermostat." He began looking through boxes on the shelves of the station and around the pit area. He opened a cabinet in the rear, but shook his head. Josie felt stifled by the smell of grease and the heat. Her arms were breaking out in a rash as they did when she was too hot or upset.

"There might be one on a wreck out back," the attendant said. "Even a damaged radiator might have a thermostat still working." He and Nathan took some tools around to the lot behind the station, where a dozen wrecked cars rusted in the weeds. Josie went to the Dairy Queen across the street and ordered a large Coke.

WHEN SHE WAS THIRTY Josie had given up hope of ever getting married. She had begun as a typist at the cotton mill office and had taken the computer courses at the county technical school when the company bought its first data processing equipment. The men treated her like one of their buddies, but no one ever asked her for a date. She often thought she had been born overweight, for no matter how much she dieted in high school and after she had never been able to get below a hundred sixty-four. Her eyes had been weak since her earliest memory. Mama said it was the poison oak that did it. When she was five and they were clearing off new ground for the garden, she had found some vines and wrapped herself in them as with boas and shawls. The next day her eyelids were swollen the size of hen eggs and her face puffed out under a rash. She had a fever of a hundred five and cried three days without stopping, Mama liked to say. They bathed her in soda water and in salt water, which made her scream even worse. When the blisters finally began to dry she picked at the scabs and started an infection. Surprisingly, the scars had disappeared from her fair skin by adolescence, but her eyes had been weakened by the poison, and she was never able to read in school until they bought her glasses. Her confidence had been destroyed by bad eyes, Mama had said, and when she started high school she looked down whenever a man noticed her. But she resented that shyness so much, that blushing and feeling silly, that she took herself in hand, and treated all boys like buddies and younger brothers. She joked and laughed with them, so they would not look at her. She could be brusque when she wanted to, and people gave in to her.

She always ate lightly at breakfast and at work. And at meal times she took no more than Mama and Daddy did. But it seemed to show on her, every bite she took. And she got especially hungry at night watching TV, and just before bedtime, and went to the refrigerator.

No one had dated her until Nathan. They had known each other for always, for he was the same age as her older brother Charles, and used to come by when she was a little girl to play baseball in the pasture or go fishing. He was six years older than she was and had never gone out with other girls. He would drive his Trans Am, and the Camaro before it, with the loud glass packs, into the church yard, and would stand outside talking with his friends until preaching would begin. He had worked as a laborer for the Abrams Construction Company, digging footings, mixing cement for the bricklayers. "He makes the best mud in the county," more than one mason had said. He would never be a mason or carpenter himself, and didn't want to be.

Nathan had been too shy to actually ask her for a date. Instead he had begun stopping by the house as though to talk to her Daddy, and then had gradually started talking more to her, until they had begun going out to the Hasty-Tasty for milkshakes, and then sometimes to movies.

Josie was glad Nathan was shy, for she had never had to make the kinds of decisions other girls had to, about how far to let a man go before you were married. Willa had told her about going to motels and parking up on the mountain with Webber before they were engaged even. But that was their business, in spite of what Mama and others said; and it wasn't quite immoral since they did get married. Other friends had told her at school and at the office about pushing boys away, and wrestling at drive-ins, and giving in because they couldn't get any dates otherwise. But that was risky because if you gave in with more than one boyfriend you might get a reputation, and no one would marry you.

She had not been immoral, and could look the preacher in the face when she said her vows. She was not a hypocrite sinning on Saturday night and teaching her Sunday School class the next morning. And she was sure Nathan had not been immoral either. He was too shy, and didn't seem to think of women in that way, except in his jokes. With her encouragement he would always be a church-going man, and she would not have to worry about pleasing him, about him stepping out with other women.

Through the window of the Dairy Queen she could see the garage man lying under the front of the car on a roller board. Nathan bent over the radiator, wiping his forehead with his sleeve from time to time. The man pushed himself out from under the car and stood up. He talked, wiping his hands on a rag. Josie paid for her Coke and ordered another for Nathan.

"That'll cost you twelve dollars," the man said.

"We're much obliged, much obliged," Nathan said, counting out the money.

"I can tell you're a good man, helping us out this way," Josie said.

"You folks have a happy trip, and a good life."

THEY WERE IN really flat country now, passing swamps and river bottoms with wide muddy edges. Some of the country was nothing but pines. Josie felt relieved and grateful. She kept looking around expecting to see mountains, but there was nothing higher than a water tank in the distance. In the late sun bugs splattered on the windshield, and Nathan turned the wipers on, and the sprayer. But the sprayer soon ran out of solution.

"I should have got more cleaner," he said.

"It don't matter. We'll be there soon," she said, and moved closer to him. Getting the car fixed did not seem to have cheered him at all. It was because he had stood out in the heat all that time, she thought. He drank the Coke in silence and flung the cup out the window.

"You'll get us arrested for littering. We'll spend the night in some dirty jail."

But he didn't respond. He looked worn out from the driving and the heat.

The air was getting even more humid, and smelled like the smokehouse on a hot rainy day. They asked directions at an Exxon station, and then drove into the entrance of the Carolina Winds just as it really got dark.

"I'll go get the key," Nathan said.

"Here, honey, let me give you some money. They'll want you to pay now." She took the envelope out of her purse and counted out the six twenties and the five.

"There'll be tax," Nathan said.

She took out another five.

While he was gone she tried to see the ocean but

couldn't. There was a gray area beyond the motel, that looked like a field of gravel, and people were walking near it. In the dark she couldn't tell much about it, except the gravel seemed to slope up to a ridge.

A man came out with Nathan to help carry the bags. As they walked through the double entrance Josie was hit by the air conditioning. It was like stepping into a deep cellar. The thick carpet underfoot seemed perfumed, and sparkled like frost on a winter morning. They walked up one flight of stairs and through a room with lots of couches and coffee tables. Everyone was looking at them. She wished she had taken off the dress at the filling station and put something casual on.

The man who brought the suitcases unlocked the door and flipped on the light. It was exactly the way Willa had said. Everything was white and the faintest pink, and matching. There must be four or five mirrors in the room, and the bed was king-size. The carpet was deep as a lawn of white mink. She hoped Nathan would carry her across the threshold, but he seemed to have forgotten. As soon as the man was gone she kissed him.

"What's wrong, honey. I've never seen you so gloomy. This is our honeymoon."

He sat down on the edge of the bed. "I'm just worn out," he said.

"Let's take a shower, and then we'll feel better. And then we can have supper."

She opened the suitcase and took out fresh clothes, and her nightie and hairbrush. Willa had advised her to buy a skimpy black negligee to tease Nathan. But she knew that was not for her. That kind of thing was for slimmer girls. Instead she had picked a shiny yellow that was not see-through.

Nathan had loosened his shirt collar and was staring at the curtained window. He was sweating more than he had outside in the heat.

"I'll just take a shower," she said, and giggled. It was the first time she had undressed near him. "We made it; we have nothing to worry about," she said. She loosened his tie and ran her finger around his ear. There was a smudge of grease on his cheek from the filling station, and she rubbed it away with a Kleenex from the fancy box beside the bed.

"What *is* it?" she said.

She had read in magazines that the bridegroom was often more nervous than the bride on the wedding night because he felt he must perform. Especially if he was inexperienced. She was prepared to be as patient as necessary.

"I'll be back," she said, glancing at him as she closed the bathroom door. He slumped in the chair.

The showerhead was adjustable, and turned like a combination lock until the water came down in a slow spring rain, the kind that really starts things growing and doesn't wash the new-plowed ground. As the whisks of water brushed her face and neck and back they seemed to carry away the wear of the hot day, soothing the rash and dissolving the salt and highway grime. When she was a girl she liked to be caught in a summer rain, and would go on playing in the garden or back yard while her face and hair were licked by the pulse of drops. It made her feel close and free, until Mama started calling her from the porch to come and dry off.

When she came out the bathroom Nathan still sat as he had before.

"That's a lot better," she said. "You should take one too. It's easier to rest if you've had a shower."

He did not answer.

"You've had a long day. You need to take a shower and then we'll go eat."

Willa had told her about the restaurant in the motel, where you could get any kind of seafood, including lobster. She didn't feel like trying lobster tonight, but she had thought off and on all day of the specialty of breaded and fried shrimp.

"Hurry up honey; don't you want some dinner?"

"No, I ain't hungry."

"Are you sick? The heat has made you sick?"

The air conditioner seemed to be muttering again. Out the window she could see the lights of the street and the darkness beyond that must be the ocean.

"You want to watch television then for a while? And then

we'll go out?" Willa had said one of the channels showed only X-rated movies.

"You want to turn it on to the dirty movies. I knowed it from the start," she said with a giggle.

"Shut up and let me think," he said.

"Think about what? This is our honeymoon, buster," she said. "Here I am and here you are, and we're married and over twenty-one. And besides, I'm getting hungry."

"There's something I didn't tell you."

"Tell me anything, you rascal. We're married."

What did he mean? That he was broke, had lost his job?

"I never developed," he said.

She had heard about men who had the mumps 'go in' on them, who were sterile, and she had read about men who were impotent.

"I just never grew," he said. "I mean like a man. I'm still a little boy there. I can show you."

"No!"

"I should have told you."

"Maybe I can help."

"No, the doctor said that wouldn't work."

"The doctor should have told me."

"I told him I already had."

"It doesn't matter."

She sat at the dresser a long time thinking. It was after midnight when she began crying, after he was already asleep in his clothes on the vibra-bed. She swore she would punish him every single day of their married lives, but knew that would bring her nothing she desired.

Later that night she woke up in the chair by the dresser. She must have gone to sleep crying, for her cheeks were sticky. Nathan slept sunk into the big bed like something fallen from a great height. At least there were some things she would not have to worry about, that other women had to. The ocean outside, or maybe the air conditioning, rumbled. She began to feel faintly hungry.

Family Land

DEW WAS SO HEAVY the weeds and spider webs in the garden seemed hung with Christmas balls. It pained her to look at the nettles between the rows of corn and okra, but at least Scottie had rototilled the baulks once since school was out. The real source of her guilt was the weeds around the squash and tomato vines, where the tiller could not reach. Scottie would do any job where an engine was used, but the hoe work and hand work were her responsibility. Daddy would help if she asked, but he had enough to do in his own garden, and driving his pickup to the rest home every day.

She tried to pull a few ragweeds at the edge without getting her moccasins wet or dirty. Her hands and forearms were quickly soaked by the shaken dew and she wiped them across her face. She had not gone to bed last night, but must have dropped asleep on the couch around two, for the last thing she remembered was Gary Cooper struck by lightning in *Sergeant York* and reforming his life. She had wakened, slumped on the cushions, at five and walked out to the garden just as the sun rose over Tryon Mountain; she'd left the patio door open in case the phone rang, or the children woke.

When she married Clint, Daddy had been silent, but she knew he disapproved. She thought it was because Clint was from town and didn't want to farm and would not attend church. She liked him for just those reasons, for she meant to work in town, to stay away from farming, and to give less time to church activities than her parents had. She shared with Clint a love of sportscars and speedboats. He was the company champion at both bowling and baseball. His favorite story was about the coonhunter who was stopped by the preacher and asked why he hadn't been attending church. "Reverend, all my dogs is saved," the hunter said.

Within a year she had admitted to herself that Daddy was right. It wasn't only that Clint had no interest in the land Daddy had deeded to them, except to sell it, nor that he refused to drop by Mama's and Daddy's even on weekends. It was the way he went off with the bowling team and the baseball team at night and on weekends, so often and so long she began to wonder if he had a girlfriend. Once he had been locked up for D & D, and she got her cousin to drive her to the jail to make bail, hoping Mama and Daddy would not find out. But of course it was printed in Monday afternoon's paper.

The weeds around the corn had grown so big they tore out the corn roots when she jerked them up. She should take the hoe and cut them off and then cover the stumps with dirt. The hoe was in the basement, but she did not want to walk back across the wet grass to get it. Two more trips across the lawn and her moccasins would be soaked and she had no other slippers to wear in the house.

As a girl she had taken care to leave her field shoes on the porch when she came back for dinner. The rest of the family wiped their shoes on the grass and stomped a few times on the porch, and went on in. She couldn't stand to wear the dirty shoes on the linoleum floor even though it was rough with grit. One of her consolations as she picked in the muddy bean rows, cool rain tapping her shoulders and back, was the thought that she could shed the clog-thick mud-soled shoes, and after washing her feet in the pan on the back porch, put on the new slippers she'd bought at Woolworths. As she bent and searched the wet rasping vines she pictured the school clothes she would buy in Greenville in August.

The phone was ringing and she threw down a weedstalk and ran to the patio, wiping her hands on her shorts. The beagle tried to jump on her as she passed the doghouse, but she brushed him away.

"Is this Mrs. Clint Forrester?"

"Yes it is."

"This is the sheriff's office. Your husband's counsel would like to talk to you."

She looked back at the patio door still open. The dog wandered in, leaving wet tracks on the carpet. The phone cord would not reach—damn the princess phone she had chosen—so there was nothing to do but motion the dog back out. Instead he came up and licked her hand.

"Mrs. Forrester, this is Doug Smith. I've been appointed to represent your husband. Could we meet and talk soon?"

"What has happened?" Her breath tightened.

"There's been some difficulty. I don't think we should talk about it over the phone. Can you meet me this afternoon?"

"I don't have a car. Can you give me some idea what's going on?"

The lawyer had spoken so calmly she felt guilty for raising her voice.

"I don't have the car. Clint took it last night bowling. Can you come down here?"

There was silence for a few seconds. "The problem is this," he finally said. "The charge is pretty serious and bail is going to be high."

"How high?"

"The judge will set that this morning. It could go as much as ten thousand."

"What is the charge?" She had difficulty saying words into the phone. The last fifteen years of her life had been leading to this moment. The dog licked her hand again and she slapped him away.

"Are you sure you want to discuss this on the phone, Mrs. Forrester?"

"I don't know what's going on," she said.

"It's a charge of molestation, sexual abuse of a minor."

"A what?"

"A nine-year-old girl."

She could not answer for a while. "I don't have that kind of money," she said.

"Then we'll have to get a bondsman. It may entail a lien on your house. You do own your house, don't you, and some land?"

She agreed to meet the lawyer in town that afternoon to settle the bond payment. Then she hung up and went out onto the patio, closing the door behind her and the dog. The sun was completely over the ridge now and the lawn flared with prisms and signalling mirrors. Stacy had left her Cabbage Patch doll out and it lay soaked by the swings. The grill smelled bitter with ashes and rancid grease. She tried to concentrate, but nothing would focus in her mind but the irritating cool voice of the lawyer. There was money in this for him. The image of a nine-year-old girl, two years older than Stacy, hovered somewhere, and she kept pushing it aside. The phone was ringing again.

It was the marina at Lake Thurmond. The boat had to be picked up today. "But I have no way to get it today," she said.

"Lady, a boat left here a week is turned over to the sheriff, just like a car."

"But I don't have the truck; it's still in the shop."

"Then you'll have to rent one." The man hung up.

Clint had taken her car last night because his pickup was still in the garage at Spartanburg. They had towed the boat down to Lake Thurmond last Saturday and the clutch went just as they reached the lake. Leaving the boat at the marina, they told the manager they'd be back by Tuesday. The truck was fixed by Monday afternoon, but the bill, including overtime and weekend rates, was more than Clint could pay, so he had to leave it there. If the boat was taken by the sheriff it would mean a fine because they had never registered it in South Carolina. She had warned Clint about the registration if he took it to Lake Thurmond.

"Who'll ever know?" he said. "I won't pay fees in two states."

STACY CAME OUT of the bedroom carrying a ragged blanket and turned on the TV.

"Can't watch until you've had breakfast, honey."

"Oh!" Stacy said, and flung the blanket across the room.

"Here, I'll fix you some cereal."

"I want an ice cream sandwich."

As she put the water on to boil, Stacy got an ice cream bar out of the freezer. She was too distracted to be strict this morning. What did it matter? When she was a girl she got ice cream at most once a week when Daddy took the truck to the market and brought each of them a cup of Biltmore ice cream with a wooden spoon sealed in wax paper. It was always melted around the edges by the time he got home, but the creamy syrup made it better. She had promised herself that when she grew up she would have ice cream every day and her children could eat all they wanted.

"Can I take my pistol down to the river?" Scottie asked from the hall door. He was already dressed.

"Are you going alone?"

"Just with Johnny and Wayne."

"Isn't that dangerous, to have it when the other boys are along?" Clint insisted on giving him the .22 pistol for his twelfth birthday. Maybe a rifle, she said, but not a pistol at his age. "He's got to know how to handle weapons," Clint answered. "Besides, this is becoming a dangerous country."

"You don't want me to do *anything* that's fun," Scottie shouted.

"It's just too dangerous." She tried to sound as business-like as she did at the office.

"Daddy will let me," Scottie said, and stalked back to his room.

She got out the phone book and was looking through the yellow pages for "Towing Services" when her Daddy came to the patio door.

"I brought you some blackberries," he said. "I got out and picked them before sun up." The berries glistened dark and fat in the pail.

"They're real pretty," she said.

"Best year for berries since '66," he said. "The stalks are bent almost to the ground above the branch."

He had always been the best berry picker in the community. When younger he'd go back to the huckleberry country at the head of the river before daylight and return with the old basket on his arm full of berries black as caviar. He picked faster and cleaner than anyone, getting only the ripe ones and keeping leaves and trash out of the pail.

"Something wrong?" he asked, setting the bucket on the table.

"No, nothing."

"Where's that young rascal?" he called down the hall to Scottie. But the boy was still sulking and didn't answer.

"How's princess?" he said to Stacy. She had the ice cream sandwich unwrapped and was watching cartoons. She did not notice her grandfather at all. His overalls were wet from the berry-picking and he stood by the door, reluctant to put his work shoes on the shag carpet.

"Daddy, sit down and have some coffee," she said. "I'm just making some."

"No, gotta run. Gotta pick this morning so I can carry off and stop in town this evening."

Daddy still said 'evening' for afternoon, and 'town' when he meant the rest home where they had placed Mama last February. It was as though he could not bring himself to say 'rest home'. A generation ago she would have stayed home and taken care of her mother. But there was no way to meet the mortgage payments, and car payments, and boat payments, if she didn't work. The trained care was better than anything she could provide or improvise. She had worked since before graduating from high school, sometimes at two jobs, but her hands, so expert on the word-processors, would be clumsy giving Mama shots and turning her on the bed for washing and the bedpan.

"I would go with you but I've got to pick up the boat at Lake Thurmond," she said. "And then I have to talk to a lawyer in town this afternoon."

"A lawyer?" Daddy fiddled with the leather string that served as a watch chain from his strap to the bib pocket.

"For Clint. He's in trouble again."

Daddy did not ask what the trouble was. He disliked Clint so much he refused to mention his name. He avoided coming to the house except when he knew Clint wasn't there, or wasn't awake.

"You can ride with me to town then," he said.

"OK, I should get back from the lake by two."

When he was gone she began calling wrecker services until she found one with a truck free to pick her up and drive down to Lake Thurmond immediately. The boat was too heavy to be pulled by a pickup. That was probably what had burned the clutch out. They had planned to get another outboard for waterskiing, but Clint liked the bigger boats so much he finally bought something between a speedboat and a cabin cruiser. "It'll save money in the long run," he insisted. "We can sleep in it and that way there'll be no motel bills and no camping out with the flies and mosquitoes." The thirty-foot boat was almost too wide for the highway lane, and it dwarfed the pickup when they hitched it on.

"You get in here and eat this," she said to Stacy, and rushed over to turn the set off and lead her daughter to the table.

"I've sugared and buttered it already."

In the old days she would have been whipped for ignoring an order. But she had not whipped either of her children since they were in Pampers. She had read in a magazine that physical punishment could actually complicate discipline in the home and make children less responsible. In different times you raised kids differently. There was a hickory tree behind the house when she was little and Daddy would go out to break a switch from it. How many times she had seen him stripping the leaves off a withe as he came back to the house, slapping the hickory on the denim of his pants. That little switch would sting her bare legs like vinegar, but it was the humiliation of the ritual that hurt most. She hated the solemnity, the role of the one who was punished. More than the bite of the hickory it was the seriousness he gave to the occasion that she felt.

What she had liked about Clint in high school was his boldness, and his jokes. He never worried what the church people thought of him. He lifted weights in the school gym during study period, and left school halfway through his senior year. She liked to feel the iron-hard biceps under his shirt, as she held his arm between classes. Once he hit her in their first year of marriage, when they still lived in the duplex in town.

"You do that again and I'll get a gun and kill you," she screamed.

"You and who else?"

"I'll use your gun," she said, remembering her Daddy's rifle was miles away.

"You'll learn to like it," he said, but never hit her again.

DADDY GAVE THEM the piece of land and they built the house in the old pepper field above the road. How enormous the seventeen-thousand-dollar mortgage had seemed in her first year at Eltrex. She typed away most of the debt in five years, but since then they had made two additions. She was sure it was now the largest house in the valley. After the boat was paid for they had meant to add a sauna and hot tub, and put up an additional garage. Clint said they should sell some land and do it now, but she had always said that would hurt Daddy too much. Not until he was dead would they sell. Lately she had begun to think Daddy was right about the land too. She would not sell a foot of the family land, and she would not put down a penny to save Clint from the law. She would tell the lawyer that.

"Scottie, I'm going to be gone till after lunch," she called down the hall. He did not answer. "Don't go off with Johnnie and Wayne. I want you here with Stacy."

She was pretty sure he would get over his sulk and do

what she said. He obeyed when he knew she really meant it. She brushed her hair and teeth and put on lipstick, then changed into a fresh blouse. Her fingers had green under the nails from the weeds, but they were smooth and slender compared to her mother's at her age. Looking at herself in the bathroom mirror she thought her legs, which had always been her best feature, were good as ever. The tan looked right against the faded cutoffs. The big wrecker drove into the yard and blew just as she was getting her purse and sunglasses.

The Lost State of Franklin

"CLOSE THAT DOOR and get back in here," John called from inside the trailer.

"Just a minute," she said over her shoulder, stressing the last word to show she would not be hurried. The soldier stood in the yard with his cap in his hands. He wore a sweater with epaulets on it, and his boots were shined.

"I don't want to bother you," he said. He seemed nervous.

"Get in here and close that door," John called again. "It's cold." John hated to be bothered when he was watching television.

She waited for the soldier to explain why he knocked. Wind swept through the field of weed stalks around the trailer and shook the old apple trees. The fallen apples touched by frost scented the wind. She leaned out the door to hear what the soldier was saying. His words were lost in puffs of vapor.

"Are you just home from over there?" she said.

"I got back last week and bought the car and drove down here," he said, motioning toward the ruby red Barracuda parked down at the road. The car gleamed in the morning sunlight, in contrast to the mud of the trail and driveway, and the beat-up pickup beside the trailer.

"What unit were you in?"

"C Company, 121st," the soldier said. He folded the cap in his hands. "I knew Doug," he said.

"You knew Doug?"

"He was my best friend. It hurt me a lot, what happened."

"Do I have to close the door myself?" John called.

She stepped down to the ground and clicked the door behind her, and stood closer to the soldier waiting for him to continue.

"I promised him I'd come see you," he said, "If something happened. And he promised me the same, that he'd go see my wife. But I'm the one that's here."

"Tell me how he died," she said. "The report just said he died in action." She was shivering in her bathrobe. She never got dressed on Saturday morning until they were ready to go to town. She pulled the collar tight on her neck. "Did he?"

"Did he what?"

"Did he die in action?"

"Well . . ."

John opened the door and stood looking at them. His glasses had slid down his nose and he pushed them up with his thumb.

"Won't you come in," she said to the soldier. She wished he had come on a weekday when John was not here. She wished she had just half an hour, just fifteen minutes, to be alone with this soldier and ask him everything about Doug in the service, in Vietnam, and the circumstances of his death.

"I don't want to bother you," he said.

"Come on in and have some coffee," she said, trying to keep her voice from trembling. Her face was already flushed. She couldn't help it when she was excited or embarrassed. Her skin was too thin, too fair. She felt like a barometer; she couldn't conceal any pressure.

John stepped aside at the last second to let her through.

The soldier wiped the mud carefully off his boots on the lower step before following her.

Inside the trailer Susan realized how it smelled of eggs and bacon from breakfast, and also of the garbage she hadn't carried out yet. Saturday was the cleaning day, and the living area and kitchen area were cluttered with bags and pizza boxes and Pepsi cans from the night before.

The television was still on loud, and she turned it down, as John plopped himself back in front of it.

"This is my husband, John," she said.

John muttered "hi" and reached out his hand, then turned back to the screen.

"Richard Link," the soldier said.

"Oh, you're the Missing Link. Doug used to mention you in his letters," Susan said. Her face felt so hot out of the wind she imagined that it was swollen.

"That's what they called me after I got lost in the jungle for two days."

"It's nice to meet you." She cleared a space on the couch, pushing aside some dirty clothes she meant to take to the laundromat.

"Won't you sit down."

"I don't want to bother you all," Link said, and glanced at John. But John was concentrating on the television.

"It's no bother. Just have a seat and I'll go warm up some coffee."

Link sat on the couch while she filled the Mr. Coffee, and there was only the sound of the game show on TV and the wind across the hill outside as it grasped the trailer and creaked the walls in gusts.

"This area was part of the Lost State of Franklin," Link said when she returned to the living area and sat down.

"The what?"

"The Lost State of Franklin. This part of the mountains was once a state formed from parts of North Carolina and Virginia after the Revolution, and declared unconstitutional. It became part of Tennessee."

"Yeah, I once heard about that in school. But I'd forgotten."

"I read a book about it, while I was stationed in Georgia."

John switched channels on the set, and turned up the volume.

Susan felt short of breath; she returned to the kitchen area for cups.

"I CAN'T COMPETE with a dead man," John had said a month after they were married, his voice quiet with feeling.

"You're not competing with anybody," Susan said.

John had found the letters in the drawer of the bureau. She had put a rubber band around them and stuck them under some socks. She didn't know why she was being secretive. Doug had been her husband after all. They had married the summer after she graduated from high school, before he was drafted. And even Doug's parents and sister did not blame her for getting married again. His mother had said it was what she needed, to not be alone, and looking ahead, not grieving for what could never be.

"Throw them away," John said. He had been looking for a cap and opened her drawer where the bundle was. He broke the rubberband and looked through the sheaf of envelopes and postcards. She didn't know why she felt guilty. There was nothing in the letters but descriptions of monsoons and names of soldiers she would never meet, names of places she heard about on TV, and always cheerful flourishes at the end such as "Don't worry about me Sugarfoot. I'm healthier than when I came here. I've probably put on more weight than you have." The postmarks were all APO San Francisco, except for the first ones from Fort Jackson when he was in basic.

John shuffled the envelopes like cards and started to open one.

"There's nothing there you need to worry about."

"They're from a dead man. I can't compete with no dead man." He threw the pile of letters on the table.

John and Doug were almost the same age and had registered at the same time. But when they were called for the physical John told the doctor about his back pains, and X-rays revealed the slipped disk. He took a job in the factory at Arden, and swallowed aspirins every day. Sometimes he had to sleep with his legs propped up on cushions, or he couldn't sleep at all when the pain flared up.

"I would have gone same as the next man," he said.

"I know that," she said. "It was just luck."

"Well he's gone and there's nothing you can do about it." John slammed the trailer door as he left.

Though she did not know what she was guilty for, for secretly keeping the letters and photograph of Doug, for holding in her heart the affection of first love, for marrying John within six months of Doug's death, she did know the guilt was a rich emotion she cultivated like a garden. The pain of the guilt kept her focused, and made her feel closer to things. Pain and sickness made her feel closer to big absolute values, such as being alive in contrast to being dead. The guilt kept her face warm and flushed, but it also gave her a balance, a poise for dealing with the dullness of living. The weight of the guilt kept her from being knocked around too lightly by John's moodiness and withdrawals. If he snapped at her she felt she deserved it, and did not brood. As he ate too much, it served her as a good warning to eat less. Her guilt kept her thin. They went out to Pizza Hut or McDonald's almost every night when they got home from work, and she felt guilty for not keeping a garden and putting up canned stuff as her mother did.

"It's the way a woman keeps a house that sets the basis of a marriage," her mother liked to say. She couldn't seem to keep the trailer picked up and cleaned up. Even if she did vacuum and straighten, the place was cluttered again in a day.

"You don't even have children yet," her mother said. "Wait till you have children tearing around and spilling."

If she had a house she would feel more like keeping it neat. The used trailer with its dirt in all the cracks and scratches in all the furniture, made cleaning seem hopeless. It was a repossessed mobile unit, and the original owners had left their mark on every foot of surface. None of the cabinets closed completely. The toilet was always stopped up. The bed sagged in the middle. John's daddy let them pull it into the field where the old orchard had been. They dug out a cess-pool, ran water from the spring on the mountain above, and set the trailer on cement blocks. Once a month the gas truck came with another tank of propane. She and Doug had promised each other they would never live in a trailer. While he went into service she stayed at home.

After John had gone, she gathered up the letters from the table and flipped through them. There was a card saying they would travel when he got out. He would take her to San Francisco and Disneyland, and the Grand Canyon. One by one she ripped the letters in half and dropped them into the garbage bag, then gathered the dishes and pans from break-fast and scraped them onto the paper. The bacon grease quickly melted through the pages, making them almost transparent. She wondered if John had found the picture of Doug she kept in her suitcase, the one she had bought for their senior class trip, or the snapshot she carried in her wal-let, underneath her driver's license.

"THE COFFEE'S READY," she said to Richard. "Do you like cream and sugar?"

"I'll take it solo."

"What?"

"Black."

If only he had come when she was alone. But then it would look as though she was going behind John's back.

"So you have read about this area of the mountains?" She handed him the cup.

"There's a lot of time for reading in the army. Also I had a great-great-great-grandfather who lived in this area after the Revolution. His name was John Peter Corn."

"You must have some kinfolks around here. I know lots of Corns."

"They would be distant ones. My ancestors moved to Georgia more than a hundred years ago."

The canned laughter from the television made it hard for her to hear him. He spoke looking down at his coffee anyway, and John had turned the volume up again.

"Maybe I should go," Richard said. "I don't want to bother you."

"No, there's no hurry," she said.

The wind bumped against the sides of the trailer and rattled the windows. The floor shuddered a little. One day this crate is going to lift right off its blocks and land in the creek, she thought. But there was no money for a down payment on a house. The money from Doug's insurance had gone for the trailer, and the honeymoon in Gatlinburg.

She waited for him to speak. This was going badly; it was slipping further in the wrong way, and there was nothing she could do about it.

"So this was the Lost State of Franklin?" she said.

"It was right at the eastern boundary of it. The line was never that clearly defined. And it didn't last long enough for careful surveying I guess."

"Must have been wild country."

"The Indians were still here."

John got up and walked past them to the refrigerator and took out a can of Pepsi. He popped it open and returned to the TV.

"You must have read a whole lot," she said.

"It's something to do off duty. The army is mostly boring, as Doug probably told you."

"Were you and him always together in Vietnam?" she said.

"Except for the time I was lost and then was in the hospital with an infected finger."

"From a wound?"

"I cut it on a can opener," Richard laughed. When he talked he gulped his words. It must be his nervousness, she thought. John turned up the sound a little more.

She could not hear what Richard was saying, and leaned closer to him.

"I got a fungus in my hand," he said.

Suddenly John stood up, and they waited for him to speak, but after a second he marched into the back of the trailer. Before she could think of anything to say he returned with his .22 rifle and sat down in front of the TV again.

"What are you doing with that thing?" she said.

"It needs a cleaning. I might go out and do a little hunting this afternoon." He opened the chamber and worked the bolt several times, flicking out cartridges into his hand.

"That thing is loaded," Susan said.

"No use to have a gun that's not loaded," John said. "Ain't that right, soldier? That what they tell you in the army?"

"Absolutely."

John flicked out all the shells and began reloading them. "I don't like your looks, soldier," he said.

"John!"

John wheeled around and faced the television. He began to polish the rifle with a sock he picked up from the floor. He turned the television up a little more and rubbed the barrel and stock of the gun as though they were covered with dust.

"I had better go," Richard said, putting the cup down on the floor. "I don't want to bother anybody."

"It's OK," she said. She knew her face was now more flushed and her voice weak.

Richard stood up and took his cap from the coffee table. "Nice meeting you," he said, but John didn't turn around. He made a gesture with his left hand, either of acknowledgment or dismissal.

"I'll walk outside with you," Susan said.

When she unlatched the door the wind whipped it back with a crash. The gust stirred pots and curtains and shelves throughout the trailer. Outside the field was washed in waves pressed and gliding through the weed stalks. Down from the frost-bitten goldenrods smoked into the wind. Cloud shadows raced across the mountainside above and dropped into the floor of the valley.

"This is some weather," Richard said. "Do you think it is going to snow?"

"It's fittified weather, as my grandma used to say."

Richard smoothed his cap and put it on, then took it off again. His car down at the road shone when a patch of sunlight passed over it.

"Well, I'll get going," he said.

"Tell me quick, did he mention me?" she said. "What did he say about me; I want to know."

WHEN SHE AND DOUG were dating they used to drive in his daddy's pickup up on Pinnacle and park. On a clear night the lights of Hendersonville seemed close, almost at their feet if they stood on the big rock on the north side. And sometimes when there was a high cloud cover they could see the glow of Asheville further on down the French Broad valley. Those were the times she remembered most from their courtship. If it was summer and they had worked in the fields, she had the glow of sunburn on her showered skin. In the cool night air her body sent out a kind of light, and she found an optimism hard to maintain at home with her sisters quarreling in their room and the floor gritty with dirt from the yard and field. They could see from the mountaintop the lights of the new GE plant out near Flat Rock, its parking lot like a landing pad or lit runway. And there was the instrument factory over near Fletcher, and lights all up and down the valleys, along the roads, where in her parents' time there was no electricity, only oil lamps and handpumps at wells, and milkcans in the springhouse.

"Ain't it pretty," she said.

"At night it is," Doug said, "When you can't see all the dirt and unpainted houses, and rusting cars in the back yards."

"Night is its own world."

He put his arm around her and his left hand under her blouse. It tickled when he touched her belly, but she had never told him so. As he worked his hand up to her breast the tickle disappeared. His fingers were rough from handling bean hampers and felt as if they had splinters that scratched her slightly.

"Night makes everything different," he said.

"Or it shows us what's really true."

"No, it covers up. There's nothing around here but hard work and no future."

"I thought I was your future."

"Except for you, there's no future."

It was sometimes when he was kissing her breasts or moving on top of her that she felt most distant, as though she was watching herself respond. Even as she enjoyed it she felt separate from the pleasure. She wondered if it was something wrong with her, if she could enjoy love as others did. She wanted to be there and beyond it at the same time. Sometimes she wished to be left alone, to her thinking and feeling. Only the desire to be with Doug was greater than her wish to be left alone. But he clashed with her moods. Just when she felt good about their plans, he reminded her just how bleak prospects really were.

"Even if you leave home, if *we* leave home, we'll want to come back, won't we?"

"I guess so," he mumbled.

"It would be fun to go somewhere like Atlanta or Florida, and make a lot of money and then come back home."

"There's sure no money here."

"But we could make it and then come back."

"Uh huh," he said. But she wasn't sure he was listening.

When they sat up on the cold seat Doug turned the radio on. She liked those times best of all, when they just sat back and listened to the radio. The weak green light of the dial was brighter than the lights in the valley below. The little window seemed like some aquarium that glowed with luminous liquid, and the needle marched across upright as a sea horse, or the tip of a rifle carried by a little soldier out of sight under the panel.

"Let's get some gospel music," she said.

"There'll be nothing but pop and mood at this hour."

"No, we can get Atlanta from up here."

He moved the knob through rock and roll on late night stations, through static and whines and chirps, and stopped on a black choir in some all night religious service.

"That's good," she said.

"You don't even like religious music."

"Sure I do. And tonight I'm feeling religious."

The gospel blues chorus came in unusually clear, as though riding some special current in the air. He turned down the volume.

"A car is coming," he said.

They saw a pair of headlights below swing in and out of sight as a car negotiated the switchbacks up the mountain. He turned the radio down even further.

"Maybe we should go," she said.

"It's just a car. Probably some coon hunters going out to Long Rock to drink."

"They may be drunk already."

"Or it might be John."

They sat silent as the lights came up the slope onto the summit, and seemed to pause on the road below them. As the vehicle went past all she could see were the headlights, and then the taillights of a pickup in the boiling dust. The truck groaned on over the mountain and then out of sight. But they could hear it chugging and rattling its sideboards on out the ridge for a long time.

"That was him," Doug said.

"He has a right to travel the road too. Look, I told him I was dating only you."

They sat in the dark for another minute, the music so faint it seemed to come from outside. Then Doug started the engine and let the truck roll down the gravel road for several minutes before turning on the lights.

"I MEAN DID HE TALK about me over there?" she said.

"Sure, all the time."

She felt her face blush hotter in the wind.

"Was he worried about me, in any way?"

"No, he just wanted to get back home. He worried about being away from home."

"And he wasn't worried about home?"

"He was most worried about the VC in the trees, and booby traps everywhere you stepped."

A shot sounded behind the trailer, a boom louder than any .22.

Richard wheeled toward the door, and then the end of the trailer.

"What was that?"

"Must be somebody hunting in the woods up there."

"That was awfully close."

"People are neighbors here; they hunt in each other's fields. It might be somebody shooting quail."

The trailer door opened and flung back in the wind, banging on the metal siding. John stood in the doorway holding the rifle.

"Who was that?" he said.

"It must be somebody hunting," Susan said.

"Was that you, soldier boy?" he asked, as though knowing it could not be Richard who had shot.

"I think it was from the woods," Richard said.

John stepped down to the ground, the rifle cradled in the crook of his arm and pointing generally toward Susan and Richard.

"You got a buddy in the woods?" he said.

They were all silent for a few seconds, Richard shaking his head.

"What a thing to say," Susan said. She looked at Richard, hoping she could reassure him in some way. She wanted to save something from the ugliness of the situation. "What a silly thing to say," she said, turning back toward John.

But he had moved to the end of the trailer and was looking at something in the field above. She followed him to see what had caught his attention.

Two men had emerged from the woods at the upper edge of the field and were working through the big weed stalks, pushing aside dead goldenrods with their elbows while holding their guns at ready. Seed down smoked from the tips of the shaken weeds, caught up in the wind like bubbles. They were not neighbors because they wore hunting suits, the kind you bought at the sporting goods store in the mall at Asheville or ordered from L. L. Bean. They looked like twins in their red and brown outfits.

"Hey!" John called, but the wind seemed to bury his voice. The hunters kept walking through the field, between the old apple trees and the woods.

"Hey you!" John called, and fired his rifle into the air twice.

"You have permission to hunt here?"

The hunters looked in their direction, said something to each other, and hurried back into the woods.

"They won't be back," John said, and laughed. "Damn town people."

"We let neighbors hunt here all the time," Susan said, turning to Richard, but he was gone. His shiny car was backing out into the road below. She ran down the trail a few yards, but it was too late. The car roared on the gravel away, leaving a tunnel of dust behind it almost as red as the hunters' hats.

"He won't be back neither," John said.

"Wasn't you the nice one."

"He had nothing to say. He just wanted some attention, or thought maybe you wouldn't be married."

She walked around him toward the trailer.

"You might as well forget," he said. "It won't do no good."

She did not answer, but pulled the door closed behind her. Richard's cup was on the floor, and she picked it up and rinsed it in the sink.

John followed her in and placed the rifle on the couch.

"And I know you're saving his picture," he said. "I saw it in your suitcase."

"You have no right to pilfer."

"It's OK; keep the damn picture."

She put the cup on the draining board and dried her hands. There was a comfort in seeing all the way to the end, even if some of the steps and accommodations for getting there were still hidden. She spread the towel carefully on the holder and went into the bedroom.

When she returned she held the large picture of Doug, and while John watched her from his chair in front of the TV she stood over the trash bag and started to tear the photograph in two. But she hesitated for a second, and then ten, and then a whole minute while John watched her. Then she carried the portrait back to the bedroom. There was still the snapshot in her wallet underneath her driver's license, but she would worry about that later.

Tailgunner

"TAILGUNNERS LOSE THEIR FINGERS, if not their lives," Baxter had said.

Jones worked his index finger inside the glove, and wiped breath fog off the bulbous window. The P-47's were peeling away, leaning to dive beneath the bombers and head back to England.

"Boys, we're on our own now," Carver said over the radio from the cockpit. "Keep those trigger fingers warm, and don't wet your diapers. We're going up."

As the B-24 began to climb Jones had a view of the blue and gray countryside. There were lakes and rivers and straight lines that might be canals or highways. He imagined he could see a column of tanks or trucks. They were almost certainly over enemy country now, and the Messerschmitts would appear any second. They always knew just where the fighter escort would use up half their gasoline and turn back.

It was a sight that always made him catch his breath, the formations of bombers behind them. The squadrons were clustered as far as he could see into the west, hundreds of ships tilting and bumping on the air currents, in waves.

Those that came back would fly further apart, since pilots often nodded off on the return journey. In the ass of each of them sat some tailgunner like himself, cramped and trying to keep his fingers warm.

"Since the most effective attacks are from the rear of your craft, the life of your crew and the success of your mission will often depend on your marksmanship, on keeping your trigger finger awake," Baxter said, slapping the chart with his ruler.

Jones slapped his gloves together and scanned the sky above the formations. Since they were near the front he would be shooting up high. The turret would get those underneath and the waist gunners those on the sides. Billy in the overhead turret and Jim in the nose might be busy today. They might be under fire for hours, because the target was far to the east, beyond Leipzig.

As the plane continued to climb Jones hoped he would not throw up. Nothing like frozen puke in your compartment. Riding backwards always made him a little sick, and the rocking on updrafts didn't help. He took off his gloves and ate another pill from the can in his hip pocket. It was already below zero, and ice was forming on the edge of the window sections. Frost crystals shone on the magazines of his guns, but they would burn away as soon as he started firing.

Though he had completed fifteen missions of his twenty-five, Jones did not expect to return home. But he did not want to die today. On every mission he prayed only to survive this trip.

"All right, let's go to oxygen," Carver said on the radio. The mask was so cold it burned his face at first, but Jones felt immediately the waking up that always came with breathing pure oxygen.

"Five o'clock, five o'clock," Jim shouted. The left waist gun and maybe the overhead opened up. But he couldn't see anything. The sky was clear behind. He flexed his fingers. His hands were cold but not yet numb. The turret and nose guns on the planes behind were firing, for he saw the sparkle of their tracers.

"One o'clock, one o'clock, Jones wake up." Bending low he could just see the Messerschmitt swing over into his field of view and start diving on them. He tilted the guns as high as they would go, but the Messerschmitt was still out of his sights. It was coming in fast, its guns sparking, and he started firing even though it was out of the line of his aim. The .50 cal. belts of ammunition looked like hands with an endless number of fingers he thought as he squeezed the trigger and the guns knocked and spat out shells. The plane started rocking, and smoke began to fill his compartment.

"Hang in there," Carver said. "We lost an engine."

The Messerschmitt swung by so close he could see the pilot's face.

When he looked back he could see they had dropped out of formation and were banking away to the left.

"We're going down," Carver called. "Everybody out."

Thrown by the fall of the plane, it was only with the greatest effort that Jones pulled himself back through the hatch into the bomb bay. The floor tilted so he could not walk but was flung along the wall.

He looked into the overhead turret and saw the glass was covered with blood and what looked like brains. McCall had been hit in the head and streamed blood into the cabin below.

The right door was open and Jones, after tightening his parachute straps, lunged into it. But the wind threw him back. Flames were reaching out of the front of the aircraft and he saw Jenkins the navigator clinging to a post just behind the cockpit. "Come on," he shouted to him.

But Jenkins was frozen to the post. He would not loosen his grip. Jones tried to knock him loose, knock him out and push him to the door, but a lurch sent him reeling backward. He clawed his way over bombs and bodies to the door and hurled himself outward. But the air pressure was like a brick wall.

The plane was spinning now, and he could do nothing but hold onto a gun mount. There was no up or down, and tools and bodies hit him as he turned over and over. The flames burned into his sheepskin jacket and through his gloves. His eyes were singed.

At that instant Jones knew all his life he had been waiting for this moment. His learning to swim in the creek, his training at gunnery school in Wyoming, his survival of typhoid fever in 1927, all led here.

Wind and flames rushed by him, and there was a great pop, as though a nutshell had broken. He was flying through smoke and oily mist, tumbling, his fingers working. He saw the clouds below rising up white and gray.

JONES LOOKED AT HIS WATCH, fifty minutes until news time. He had chosen the charcoal watch face with gold hands over a digital. He liked to buy the newest things, but in this one little thing he would be old-fashioned. There was time to go for a walk, or he could watch half a movie on the VCR. Lorna had bought him his own copy of *Twelve O'Clock High* for his birthday. He had seen it a number of times over the years, originally at a theater in Spartanburg, then on late night TV cut up for commercials. But he never tired of the opening sequence where Dean Jagger bicycles out to the abandoned air field and looks around at the hangars and control tower, and the grass at his feet begins to ripple in wind that becomes the backwash of a B-17 warming up as the film flashes back to the war.

The pain in his chest was bad today. He should take another Advil before starting on the walk. First he would have a couple of soda crackers with margarine on them for energy. That was stretching his diet, but only by the tiniest fraction. And Lorna would not be back from her meeting until six. He munched the crackers as he stepped outside.

When they bought the house, the development was at the edge of open country. Now there were new houses with carports and wooden fences all the way down the road, and they were building more out where the fields had been bulldozed into sandy lots. He had to walk past the construction to reach the country, and he resisted the curiosity to look at the framing going up. Thirty years in construction had been enough. He was ready to quit even if he had not had the heart attack. They did not even *build* houses anymore, but just knocked together sections already assembled at a factory.

He had not held a hammer in two decades when his heart put him in early retirement.

But it was only in the last few days that he had realized, while he was walking, that he had not been happy since he quit working with his hands.

"It's your nerves, from the war," Lorna explained, when he was depressed. But he never showed anyone else his depression as he rose from carpenter to foreman to supervisor and finally to vice president. Jones was the sunny one, always chewing gum, smiling, as he looked over blueprints and readouts. He was their best contact man, for lunches with prospective clients, soothing irate homeowners on the telephone after their wiring was found defective. It was something he had learned in the Air Corps and prison camp: at the worst moments, when everything seems to be going to hell, you just smile and act like a screw maybe needs tightening, or there is a slight mistake in the column of figures which you can go over and correct.

He wished he had not eaten the crackers, for the soreness under his ribs grew as he walked past some kids tinkering with an off-the-road three-wheeler. A kid about ten was red-faced from pulling the starter cord. They stood back as Jones bent over the engine. The scent of the flooded carburetor affected him like smelling salts. He pushed back the choke all the way and held it, telling the kid to pull again. The spark caught on the second try, and the engine fired and puffed out blue smoke. He flicked the choke down and it roared into a steady normal rhythm. Without looking back at him the boys climbed on the machine and sputtered away.

The smell of gas on his hands made him faintly nauseous. He tasted the margarine, rancid in his throat.

"The Thomas appetite will kill you," Lorna liked to say. It was an old joke in the family. His mother was a Thomas and her folks liked to brag about their relish for rich food. Grandpa Thomas was supposed to have killed himself eating molasses and butter on biscuits. They referred to "the Thomas appetite" as though it were some special talent, an inherited giftedness, a blessing of luck.

There was the scent of new lumber from the last construction site on the road, and he paused to inhale the fumes of fresh pine, hoping they would make his chest feel better. But the pain had increased, and his stomach was restless. He continued on the level road, glad there was nothing to climb even though he still missed the broomsedge and pasture hills of the mountains. They had moved to Sumter to be closer to Alva and the grandchildren. It would never seem like home.

He turned off the road, stepping through weeds and sandspurs, and entered a stretch of pine woods half a mile from the development. In two or three years the grove would be knocked down and covered with houses. But it was one of his favorite spots. He liked to walk out there and just stand beneath the pines, listening to the sigh in their tops, like the sound of a distant ocean. In the shade of the pines he felt more himself, as though he was closer to a self he had lost in the war and never recovered. But there was a way he felt in the pine woods that reminded him of moments in the war, as well as of childhood. It was as though he had forgotten something about himself for almost forty years. He could not explain why the peacefulness of the trees reminded him of instants of great danger and sickness, why he felt close to some bedrock definition, some value. It was just a little stand of woods. He looked up at the green canopy swaying like a lake surface. He had once stood in a similar forest in Germany, after his release.

The roar of the three-wheeler took him by surprise, and he jumped aside from the path as the boys blasted past. Their laughter reverberated above the engine noise, and they disappeared down the trail, leaving the fumes of burnt oil. The tires had torn the needles loose on the trail, and he kicked at the cleat-moulded dirt. It was almost news time.

"You've been eating margarine," Lorna said as he came in.

"How do you know?"

"You left it on the table. Do you think I'm a fool?" She was emptying the dishwasher and starting to boil things for supper. He turned on the news and sat down in the living-room. If he sat still long enough the pain in his chest might quiet down.

"Are we going to Tampa?" Lorna called from the kitchen.

"To Tampa?"

"To the reunion. I saw the newsletter," she said, wiping her hands as she came into the livingroom.

"Would you want to go? That's really for pilots and co-pilots and navigators. There won't be any non-coms there. I was just a tailgunner, remember."

"And you amounted to more than any of your squadron."

"The rest of my squadron was killed."

"The Ninety-second Bombardment Group should be proud of you. You should go and see them again."

He had only begun getting the newsletter this year. It was an accident that he knew about it. An old buddy he had run into at Columbia had told him about the Memorial Association.

"Fame's Favored Few!" it said on the cover. He read the letters and looked at the snapshots of bombardiers and radio-men sent in. But he would feel embarrassed at a reunion, a tailgunner hobnobbing with officers, listening to a lot of lies and stories he had heard before.

"I want to go," Lorna said.

It amazed him to think he had been married to Lorna for forty years. Their wedding was just something that happened to him when he got back after the war, underweight and dazed. He had never planned it, or thought it would last. He had always assumed he would eventually marry someone else more suited to him. Yet in her way she was a good person. Alva had come and grown up and married, and they were still together. The years had come and most of them were gone.

As HE FELL into the German cabbage patch, Jones saw the woman out of the corner of his eye. He was drifting sideways fast in the wind, and she broke into a run toward where she thought he would land. And when he hit and rolled over, tangled in the chute lines, she stood over him, not with a hoe or pitchfork, but a long knife. It was October and she was cutting cabbage.

"*Achtung, achtung,*" she shouted, and held the knife over him. At the moment he didn't feel the pain of the broken collar bone more than he might have noticed a hangnail. Instead he smelled the smoke on his hair and leather flightsuit, the singe of flesh and scorched oil, burned powder. In the damp air he stank like an incinerator.

His hands and clothes were smeared with the mud of the cabbage patch, a dark mud he saw was mixed with cow manure and human dung.

"*Achtung, achtung,*" the fat woman shouted and pointed toward the end of the field with the knife. He reached to unbuckle the harness, but she shook her head and tapped him on the shoulder with the blade. She assumed he was trying to reach inside the flightsuit for a pistol.

Gathering the cords of the chute in one hand she chopped them with the knife and pointed to the village beyond the field. He stumbled through the wet cabbages and mud dragging the loose ends of the harness and lines, and the woman followed, pointing her knife at his back. He had lost a glove somewhere in the fall and his right hand was cold, though not frozen.

In the village the woman turned him over to what must have been a policeman, an old man in a black uniform who locked him in a cellar while he made phone calls. It was just as damp as in England, and colder. The air in the basement seemed filled with mold and the fumes of rotten grease. His shoulder was beginning to hurt. He wondered if he would be shot. Luckily this was the countryside and had not been bombed. Just at dark a van came and took him to a prison in a large house, almost a castle.

"You will wash up here," the guard said in perfect English, and showed him to a sink in a kind of closet. After he had washed his hands and face and wiped the mud off his suit he was led upstairs into a kind of office. An officer in a red-trimmed uniform sat behind a gleaming desk.

"Good evening, and welcome to Germany," he said, and

pointed to a chair. Jones sat down, and found his knees shaking.

"Don't be afraid," the officer said. "You have nothing to fear. The Reich respects all warriors."

He was questioned in exactly the way his sergeant in gunnery school had told him he would be. After he gave his name, rank, and serial number the officer asked what unit he belonged to.

"Nothing to say," Jones said, his jaw trembling. His shoulder was hurting worse now.

"Don't worry; we know you're in the Ninety-second Bombardment Group, 325th Squadron, stationed at Bedfordshire. Am I right?"

Jones did not answer. The carpet on the floor was the color of a ruby, and sparkled in the lamplight. The officer referred to a stack of small file cards.

"We know you come from Henderson County, North Carolina," he said. "And we know you were born in 1924, and attended gunnery school in Caspar, Wyoming. Your father is named Cyrus Jones."

"Then why bother to ask?"

"We know a lot about American soldiers, especially fliers." The officer stood up. "Get out," he said. "You're useless to us. Someone will fix your shoulder in the camp."

THE DAYS IN THE PRISON CAMP never ran together. He arrived on October 3, 1944 and worked out a calendar in his mind that extended far into the next year. Each day was its own battle. It was cold and damp, and all they got to eat were potato peelings and a kind of soup made of old cabbage and other kinds of leaves. He could not explain why the months went easier for him than for many others. While other boys were cracking up and hanging themselves, talking disjointedly of home, or telling silly stories with bravado, he listened to the bombers going over every day and at night watched the fires on the horizon in the direction of Darmstadt. He was astonished to be alive after the fire and explosion. He hadn't expected to survive anyway. He wrote two or three letters for the Red Cross to deliver home, but got none in return. He expected to someday panic and run for the fence and be shot, but never did. When others were weeping in their bunks or talking with strange expressions on their faces he sat quietly or played another round with the soiled cards. When you think it's bad, he told himself, just remember, it can get a *lot* worse.

The Third Army liberated them in May, and Patton himself came by in a jeep and saluted them. Jones felt less euphoria than the others. It was a peculiar day. The soldiers lined the guards up at the gate of the compound and walked each prisoner by them. The big sergeant with the New York City accent held his .45 and asked of each, "Did he treat you good? Did this one?" Jones said they all treated him well. But when a man behind him said a guard had hit him with a rifle butt the sergeant put the Colt to the German's head and shot him on the spot, blood and brains spraying over the others. The former guards never flinched, never begged for mercy, never responded to threats or questions.

THE ANCHORMAN WAS TALKING about the position in the polls of all the presidential candidates. Jones could hardly tell the candidates apart. Then there was a report on Nicaragua, and one on the Palestinians. He wondered if there was any good news anywhere in the world. Yet he watched the news devotedly every morning and evening. Perhaps it was what people did now instead of praying. His uncle Jennings, back in the mountains, used to go out and pray in the feedroom of the barn. "Jen is out there talking to the cows and corn meal," his Daddy would say.

He concentrated on the soreness under his ribs, and the hunger that seemed to come from every cell and bone of his body. When he was hungry he was hungry all over.

"Did Alva call?" Lorna asked.

"Not while I was here."

Alva had been calling less in the past few weeks. They both knew it was not because of the land, that she was busy working as an aide in Jimmy's school. But they waited for her calls. They had moved to Sumter from Spartanburg when he retired, to be with her and the grandchildren.

The land was Jones's share of the homeplace back in the mountains. He should have sold it long ago.

"Daddy, we just want to build a summer place up there, a little house to use on weekends and in summer to escape the heat. You and Mama could stay there."

He couldn't explain why he hesitated. He almost never went back there, even in summer. The pasture had grown up in blackberries and black pines. The old log barn had caved in and been swallowed by the brush and honeysuckle. The plum trees and apple trees of his granddaddy's orchard were surrounded by tall thin pines. And his cousins seemed like strangers. They represented everything he had tried to get away from and forget: the church quarrels, the ignorant disputes about theology, the suspicion of outsiders, the money grubbing of some and the embarrassing poverty of others, the beat-up pickup trucks and the dirty children. Yet at times he ached to be back there.

There was no reason for him to deny Alva and Steve a weekend house on the old place. And yet, he hesitated.

"Everything will be yours, in time," he had said.

"They just want to build a little place," Lorna said.

"If you don't want us to do it, we sure won't," Alva said. She was hurt, and it hurt him to have hurt her. And there was no reason not to give the place to her now. And yet he did not do it.

"I want the kids to get to know the mountains, to love the place where you grew up and talk about so much," Alva said.

They did not quarrel any more about it, but she came over less often these days. And on Sundays she and Steve took the kids to McDonald's or somewhere instead of bringing them for dinner after church.

"You still want to go back there," Lorna had said.

"I do not."

"You fantasize going back to that awful place," she said. "I know you better than you know yourself."

"I left there, remember?"

"You want to go back there and get in a boundary dispute with one of your fine cousins. Nothing else will satisfy you."

He leaned closer to the television, hoping she would go back in the kitchen.

"You want to buy a pickup truck and drive in the mud up the mountain and down along the creek. And you want two shotguns in a rack on the back window."

"And what do you want?"

The fever around his heart was spreading into his shoulder and down his left arm. He had walked too far. And the dirt vehicle had surprised him. He would have to sit still for two or three days, before he started exercising again.

"She can have the land for whatever she wants," he said. "I just want her to wait a while, until we see what interest rates are going to do."

"You want to go back there and scratch in the mud. You'd still be there if I hadn't pushed you after the war."

THE DAY HIS PARENTS RECEIVED THE TELEGRAM from England saying he had been shot down, they called a prayer meeting at their house. Lorna and her parents had come. He had dated her a little in high school, and written her a few times from Bedfordshire, and got a cake from her at Christmas.

And the day he returned home after the war her parents had driven up to the house with a box of cookies she had made. "Lorna is at home waiting for you," they said.

It had happened as fast as water running downhill. The engagement, the wedding, the first carpentry job in Greenville with her father. He never worked on the farm again. He bought a new rifle but never took it hunting. Instead they drove up every year for Homecoming in a new car. When Alva was growing up they brought her along in sunsuits to play with her cousins, warning her to watch out for snakes in the weeds and mud along the branch.

The TV was too loud, and he leaned forward to turn it down. The thud underneath his ribs must have shown on his face.

"Are you OK?" Lorna said.

"I just walked too far. I'm a little tired."

"I'll get your pills."

"No, no, I'm all right."

"You don't look all right."

The blaring of the TV, and her hovering over, made him want to shout. As he used to at board meetings when he had to get his way. But that was the worst thing he could do now, get any more worked up.

"We'll call up Alva and take them all out for dinner tomorrow, to the Western Steer," he said.

"You may not feel up to it. You've gone and given yourself another attack, charging out on walks, like you want to kill yourself."

Lorna had never understood the sharpness of her tongue. It was a habit she had developed as a teenager, and it had grown on her over the years. She did not realize how she sounded. He had thought of recording her on tape and then playing it back to her. She would be astonished at the harshness in her voice, at the belittling tone of her comments. She knew how to be polite in public, and with her friends from church. It was only with him, and with her sisters, that side of her came out. But she was mostly a good woman, though he had not meant to spend his life with her. That was why he seemed so tolerant, why he almost never quarreled. If he let himself go who knows what he would end up saying. He might let it out that he had never wanted to marry her, never wanted to be with her. It would tear away whatever grace their life had had, pull down the scaffold and show how badly fitted and supported they really were. It would ruin her opinion and pride in herself. His very lack of feeling for her had been the essence of his devotion and patience, which so many friends had praised, especially at the times when other friends had divorced.

"I'll go get your pills," she said.

"No, it's just a little heartburn. I shouldn't have eaten the margarine."

"I don't like your look. You'd better take something before it gets worse."

"OK, I'll take just one."

BY THE TIME the news was over he had begun to feel better.

"Do you really want to go to the Ninety-second reunion?" he asked as they sat down to eat.

"Sure, I'm tired of staying home." She served up a helping of tuna casserole. "And we could go on down to Miami or Key West afterward."

"I was thinking we might invite Alva and Steve and the children to come along."

"Do you think they would be interested? I mean they won't know anybody there."

"We could stop at Disney World."

"I don't think they are interested in World War Two stuff. You know how the young are."

He had never talked much about the war to Lorna and Alva. When he first got back everyone asked and he did not want to try to describe or explain the explosion, and the months in the prison camp. And when he met the overhead gunner's mother in Washington, D.C., on the way home, he could not tell her he had seen McCall's blood and brains sprayed all over the glass dome. Instead he told her only that McCall had died instantly of a direct hit and felt no pain, which was probably true. At least he didn't know that the screams he had heard behind him were McCall's.

Twenty years later, when he decided he wanted to talk about the war, no one was interested. In 1965 nobody, at least of Alva's generation, cared about that war. And he was too busy to think about it much, except that he did relive moments when he was alone. At times he caught himself flexing his trigger finger, and visualizing the two barrels of his guns spitting tracers. The .50 caliber fingers stretched far out into the stratosphere to touch an attacker. It was the miracle that he had survived, he alone, that kept coming back to mind. There must be some purpose for which he had been spared, but he didn't know what it was. "You are sitting in the hind-end of death," Baxter liked to say, "And it's cold there."

If there was any one image from the war that kept coming back to him in the last few weeks it was the mud. The base at Podington in Bedfordshire was nothing but ruts and puddles except for the paved runways and parking circles. It rained every day, and water stood in pools in front of the mess halls, the motorpools, the Quonset barracks. Even the smell of the mud came back to him, a slightly burned, faintly rotten smell. Maybe the area had once been a dump for ashes, for charcoal. The countryside was green, even in winter, but everywhere a jeep or truck or foot had touched was sucking, slurping mud. The base was so vast you couldn't see the end of it, except for the miles of B-17's and B-24's lined up for take-off in the early morning. It was only when they got into the air that he could look back and see the shape of the place, the huge central runway and the turnaround loops through the green fields, and the clusters of buildings. If the cloud cover was high enough he could always see the clock face on the village church as they started climbing.

The mud and the waiting were the real facts of the war. The mud in the prison compound had bits of brick and cement in it, probably rubble from bombed buildings. The mud was brown, and smelled like the latrines. It was worked and churned by hundreds of feet in the enclosed space. In the spring of 1945 they had to put down boards and sections from crates to walk on.

Since his retirement he had remembered that waiting, and felt a boredom he was ashamed of. If it were not for his heart he would go back to work.

"You'll enjoy talking to the others," Lorna was saying.

"They'll all be pilots, flight officers. I remember what buddies they were."

"There will be other gunners."

"Tailgunners don't go to reunions."

"You can take your uniform. I'll get it out of the cedar chest."

He felt a pressure building in his torso, like the push of a basketball under water trying to rise. He put his finger over his mouth and belched.

"Are you all right?" Lorna said. "I'll get another pill."

WHEN JONES CAME TO he was floating through a cloud of smoke and burned oil. He heard wind, and the sound of airplane motors far away. The air underneath was pressing him.

As he realized he was falling he automatically reached for the ripcord D-ring and found it. The cord was partly burned but he yanked it and felt the jerk of the blossoming chute. The plane had exploded and thrown him free. The wind fluttered and the clouds below gave way as he plunged through. It occurred to him he might be dead and this was his journey into heaven or maybe hell. The steam and smoke coiled around him, and something fell past, a piece of wing or rudder. If this was death he was too numb with cold to feel anything. His trigger finger was stiff. He remembered the pool in the creek where he had learned to swim, and the drawing paper they used in gunnery school to describe a trajectory. There was the smell of the schoolhouse on the first day of the new year, the puke smell of glue on the new books and scent of oil on the floors. He had seen a Santa Claus once in a store window in Greenville where they had gone to the dentist. The Santa Claus had electric eyes that winked. He could remember the instant he was brought up out of the river at his baptizing, and the way light and time had started again after the shock of the cold water. There was a smell in the front room of his Grandma's house, a mixture of mothballs and mildew and flowers. The clouds opened underneath and he could see the terrain swelling closer, into focus, and the miracle was it wasn't heaven at all but a muddy German cabbage patch he was floating into.

The Half Nelson

THE SQUEALS coming from the trailer could be heard two hundred yards down the road. There were screams and shouts, then a long groan. "Oh my god, Oh my god," drifted out on the late evening air.

"Sounds like Liddy is enjoying herself," Charles said.

"Never saw anybody who loves wrestling that much," Virginia said.

The road was deserted in that spell just before dark. When there was a pause in the noise from the trailer the crickets in the weeds above the bank could be heard like timing devices going off at random.

"Have there been many katydids this year?" Charles said.

"You'll hear a rage of them when it gets good dark," Virginia said. "A hot summer brings them out."

"One of the things I miss in California is katydids."

"Then you should move back," Virginia said.

"I can't quit my job and move back just to hear the katydids."

"Me and Frank are not getting younger." It was an old

argument between them, whether he should move back to the mountains at all costs so the children could be near their grandparents.

Bats shushed in the air above them, swooping for moths. There was clapping from the trailer just ahead.

"I hate to disturb them," Charles said. "Saturday night wrestling is sacred."

"They'll be happy to see you," Virginia said.

When he opened the door Liddy was clapping again. Her chair had been moved close to the TV and the walker stood in the middle of the room. Alvin sat on the couch paring his nails with his pocketknife as he watched the match.

"Good gracious," Liddy said when she saw Charles. "I didn't know you was home." Her face was flushed and sweaty. Since the stroke she had not been able to walk without the walker, but he noticed she had gained weight since he was home at Christmas.

"How do," Alvin said. "Pull up a chair."

"We can't stay but a minute," Virginia said. "Charlie's flying back in the morning."

"When did you come?" Liddy said. She took her eyes off the screen for a second.

"I got in last night."

"He went to a meeting in Atlanta," Virginia said. Charles's investment company had its main office in Los Angeles, but management had decided in recent years to have meetings at regional offices in Denver, Atlanta, and Boston.

"How long a flight is that?" Alvin said, looking at each of his nails.

"Back to L.A.?"

"About six hours," Virginia said. She sat down on the couch beside Alvin and was watching the screen. A single lamp by the door was turned on, but the room was mostly lit by the flicker from the set.

Charles pulled a kitchen chair closer to the center of the room, careful to stay out of Liddy's line of sight. Two huge men were circling in the ring and two others watched from outside the ropes. One of those in the ring wore a blond wig that looked debutantish above his massive glistening shoulders. His opponent wore a mask and black tights.

The masked man pushed the other against the ropes and hit him in the chest.

"That's the mean one," Liddy said. "The man in the black suit, that's the Great Bolo."

The man on the ropes tried to duck the Great Bolo's blows, and using the spring of the ropes leapt over his adversary's head.

Liddy clapped and laughed.

"Who is the other man?" Charles said.

"That's Palomino George," Alvin said, folding his knife and putting it in his pocket.

"Who's winning?" Virginia said.

"Nobody yet," Liddy said. "It's a tag team."

The blond man whirled around and caught the masked man's right arm. Before the Great Bolo could respond he was jerked around and around. He flailed his free arm as though he was giddy.

"The Bolo fights dirty," Alvin said. "He likes to hurt people."

Palomino George flung the Bolo against the ropes, and it looked as though the masked man was beaten. But he sprang back and rammed the blond man in the chest with his head.

"He's got a head like a wrecking ball," the announcer was saying. The referee skipped around the ring, bending to look close at the holds and then backing away.

"The Bolo ain't hardly human," Alvin said.

While Palomino George was down the Bolo took one of his feet in his hands and, placing his shoe on George's other leg, twisted the foot while George writhed and beat the mat with his elbows.

"He's got him, he's got him," Liddy shouted.

"It's a rough sport," Alvin said to Charles.

But while he was banging the mat in agony Palomino George was inching toward the ropes, and suddenly his partner, who stood just outside the ring, reached through and tagged him. The partner, who wore braids and a feather behind his head, jumped over the ropes and hit the Great Bolo in the ribs. Palomino George escaped from the ring. The crowd was on its feet cheering.

"Everybody likes Palomino George and don't nobody like the Bolo," Liddy said.

"Who's his partner?" Charles said.

"That's Cherokee McGee. Sometimes he goes crazy and gives his Indian yell. Then nobody can stop him," Alvin said.

"And he does a war dance too," Liddy said.

The two wrestlers were jumping over each other's heads by turns.

"Aw he's not going to do his war dance yet," Alvin said, and leaned back on the couch.

Outside it was almost completely dark. The sky through the window looked a deep ink blue. But watching the television had ruined Charles's dark-adjusted eyes.

"What did the doctor say?" Virginia said to Liddy.

"Said it was high but not high enough to put me in the hospital."

"Said the blood pressure was over two hundred," Alvin said, taking his pocketknife out again and opening it.

"That's pretty high," Virginia said.

"Said he thinks it's the old arthritis medicine that's keeping it up," Liddy said.

"Then he ought to take you off it."

"Said he's afraid then I couldn't walk at all," Liddy said, her eyes back on the screen. The Great Bolo's partner had tagged into the ring and was circling Cherokee George.

"That's Hurricane Heaney," Alvin said, smoothing the edges of his nails with the knife blade.

Hurricane Heaney had red curly hair and a red face. His nose looked as though it had been broken a number of times. His shoulders were even wider than Palomino George's, but he was not as tall. He and Cherokee McGee galloped around each other like binary stars about to collide.

"You better watch that blood pressure or you'll go like Vince," Virginia said.

"Did you go to the funeral?" Liddy said, turning away from the screen for an instant.

"No, but I went to the visiting hours," Virginia said.

"How did he look?"

"They didn't open him up."

Hurricane Heaney had picked up Cherokee and pressed him over his head. He ran around the ring showing his prize, while the crowd booed.

"People in Charlotte sure like Palomino George and Cherokee," Alvin said. Hurricane threw Cherokee down on the mat.

"Ouch!" Liddy cried, and then laughed at herself.

"No, Sue didn't want him opened at all," Virginia said. "She didn't want people to see how bad he looked in his final days."

"That emphysema is bad stuff," Alvin said.

"Poor Vince got down to eighty pounds," Virginia said.

"I heard it was pneumonia that really got him," Liddy said.

"His lungs just filled up. You could say he drowned," Virginia said.

Charles looked at his watch. He could no longer see the sky beyond the window. The glass reflected the light from the television.

"Sue did all she could for him. She sure did her part," Virginia said. "For more than two years she took care of him like a baby."

"I heard he got a lot of bedsores near the end," Alvin said.

"They couldn't tell if it was bedsores or some kind of infection breaking out. But they say he was just covered."

"Hit him, hit him!" Liddy shouted. The Bolo had entered the ring again and was twisting Cherokee McGee's arm behind his back.

Cherokee wheeled and slugged the masked man, and Liddy clapped.

"There at the end Sue couldn't even wash him because of the sores," Virginia said. "She more or less had to pour water over him. I can't hardly bear to think about it."

"Only the Lord understands," Alvin said, and folded up his knife again.

Cherokee McGee tagged Palomino George, and the wigged giant slid into the ring. He began to run in place, stepping high as a drum majorette.

"Now the Bolo's going to get it," Liddy said.

"How is Jimmy?" Charles said.

After three or four seconds Alvin turned away from the screen. "Ain't seen him in three weeks," he said.

There was a flicker at the window. At first Charles thought it was a reflection from the television, but the flash came again and he saw it was heat lightning. For an instant he could see the sky behind the pines, and the outline of a chicken resting on a limb.

"He's still working in Greenville?" Charles said.

"They sent him on down to Augusta. They're building a shopping mall down there. He's talking about moving to Augusta."

"I thought Jimmy was going to build a house up here and quit construction," Virginia said. "I thought he wanted to start a nursery down by the branch."

"He does want to move back when he can," Liddy said. "But it will take a while to save enough."

"He wants to sell real estate," Alvin said. "I think that's what he wants to do."

As Palomino George continued his high-stepping dance the Great Bolo circled, jabbed and feinted. Palomino stepped faster, turning to face his opponent. The crowd began cheering. "This promises to be a turning point in the fight," the announcer said.

"Now he's going to get him," Liddy cried, her face shining. Her face streamed in the muggy darkness. Everything in the room seemed to glisten with moisture, in the light from the screen. The trailer smelled of hot electric circuits and plastic.

"He just keeps on dancing," Virginia said.

"He's revving up to attack," Alvin said.

"He always does that before he makes his final push," Liddy said.

The huge man in the blond wig ran so hard his legs were a blur.

"Now the Bolo will get it," Alvin said.

The Bolo circled, back to the ropes, then lunged for Palomino. But the giant stepped aside and the masked man fell forward stumbling all the way to the corner as the referee ran out of the way. Just as the Bolo touched the ropes his partner tagged him and jumped into the ring.

"Oh heck," Liddy said. "The Bolo is such a coward."

"He done all that dancing for nothing," Alvin said.

"Can't he whip Hurricane just as well?" Virginia said.

"But people likes Hurricane," Alvin said. "It's not the same as beating the old Bolo."

Liddy was quiet as Palomino and Hurricane grappled and the referee circled them. Hurricane tried to get a half nelson on the powerful neck.

"Palomino, don't let him do it," Liddy shouted.

But the sense of crisis had gone out of the match once the Bolo left the ring. There was a feeling of let-down in Liddy's gestures. The crowd had changed, as though a chemical reaction had taken place.

"Is the church going to give anything to Sue?" Alvin said. Virginia was the treasurer of the church.

"We made up more than five hundred dollars," Virginia said.

"She must owe a hundred times that much at least," Liddy said.

"They must have some insurance, and Medicare," Alvin said.

"What Sue needs is a vacation," Virginia said. "She's had two long years. She's such a little woman, and she had to lift him all those times, in and out of bed, on the bedpan. And him covered with them sores."

"I'm sure the Lord knows what he's doing," Alvin said. "But some folks sure does suffer."

"I thought Vince had a lot of friends," Virginia said. "But Sue said almost nobody ever came by to see him."

"He was sick too long. I stopped by a few times, but he just laid there and couldn't talk above a whisper," Alvin said.

"The young don't have time to visit," Liddy said.

"He sure would have liked to see Charles," Virginia said. "But Charles was two days too late."

"How is your garden?" Alvin said to Virginia.

The heat lightning flashed again, and Charles thought he could hear a rumor of thunder.

"Looky, looky, looky," Liddy cried. "They're all going to get into it."

The Bolo and Hurricane had Palomino down on the mat, each one twisting a foot. But Cherokee McGee climbed over the ropes and onto Hurricane's back, riding him like a rodeo bull and giving war whoops. The referee's shouts were ignored.

Liddy raised herself up on her elbows, and dropped back into the chair, clapping. Alvin leaned forward from the couch.

"Now they're going to get it," Liddy said.

"I didn't know they could all be in there at the same time," Virginia said.

"They're not supposed to," Alvin said. "But when they all get going nothing can't stop them."

Cherokee slapped Hurricane on the side of his head, as though he was scolding a willful horse. Hurricane slammed into the corner of the ring, trying to dislodge his rider. But Cherokee grabbed the ropes and pulled them both down.

Hurricane held his knee where it had crashed on the mat, grimacing with pain. Cherokee pushed him flat with his foot and dropped on top of him, trying to pin the shoulders as the referee hovered nearby.

Just then the Bolo wrenched free on the other side of the ring and leapt on top of Cherokee. The Indian rolled over howling with pain, as Palomino jumped on all three of them.

"I just can't look," Liddy shrieked.

The referee tried to separate the kicking and twisting bodies. Suddenly Palomino tore free and dropped straight on the shoulders of Hurricane, putting his neck in the vise of a half nelson. Cherokee and the Bolo were rolling over and over each other around the mat. The crowd was on its feet cheering as the referee blew his whistle. Palomino relaxed his hold and allowed the referee to raise his right arm as he got to his feet. The crowd roared.

"Let's see if the Bolo will shake hands," Alvin said.

The Bolo and Cherokee had stopped rolling and stood glaring at each other, as Cherokee raised his arm in victory also. The referee motioned for all the wrestlers to shake hands, but the Bolo shook his head and walked to the other side of the ring. The crowd booed.

Hurricane got to his feet and shook with Palomino and Cherokee, then slipped through the ropes. But the Bolo walked from one side of the ring to the other, shaking his fist as the crowd booed him. He would not leave the ring until Palomino and Cherokee did. As a commercial came on Alvin switched off the set.

"The Bolo is too arrogant to take losing," Liddy said. Charles could not tell if she was slightly embarrassed for having been so caught up in the fight, or if she was exhausted by the excitement.

"She's not supposed to watch wrestling," Alvin said. "It sends her blood pressure up too high."

"I'll miss it for a couple of weeks anyway," Liddy said. "While I'm in for the tests."

Virginia looked at Alvin and then at Charles in the weak lamplight. "You're going in for tests?" she said.

"They just want to do some more tests," Liddy said.

"They think it might be her gall bladder or kidneys driving the blood pressure up," Alvin said.

"When do you go in?"

"On Tuesday."

"They said it might be for ten days, two weeks at most," Alvin said.

"Let me know if there's anything I can do to help," Virginia said.

The katydids in the trees outside seemed to get louder suddenly. "You know it's almost fall when you can hear them like that," Alvin said.

"We've got to go," Virginia said. "We're liable to step on a snake in the dark."

Charles stood up, his left foot partly asleep. He put his weight on the right.

"So you fly back in the morning?" Alvin said.

"Early in the morning, to Atlanta and then to Los Angeles."

"You like to ride them big airplanes?" Alvin said.

"I don't mind them much anymore."

"He flies all the time," Virginia said.

"Good luck with the tests," Charles said as they slipped out the door into the dark.

The crickets were still busy in the grass of the yard, but were drowned out by the chorus of katydids in the trees nearby which seemed to be answering another chorus up on the ridge. Their dialogue sounded vivid enough to be translated, if one knew the terms.

Heat lightning still flashed off to the southwest, but looking toward it only made it harder to see the ground again.

"Let's stay in the middle of the road," Virginia said. "Snakes are crawling blind this time of year."

"Don't stumble on the gravel," he said, holding onto her arm. "Our eyes will be adjusted to the dark soon."

Night Thoughts

THE NURSES WERE all drunk again. Those who came in for the night shift waited until Reverend Sams and Mrs. King the head nurse left at five o'clock, and then they started the hell-raising. First they brought around the supper, on trays so warm they must have been in the oven, sent from somewhere else and just heated up. They didn't expect you to eat the stuff, but they brought it anyway, the creamed corn, the apple sauce, the custard, soft things for old people without teeth. And the coffee, too hot to drink for thirty minutes in the styrofoam, tasted like boiled spunk water. But at least it *was* coffee, and it was all she usually had from the tray. Then they brought around the medication in little paper cups and turned the lights down everywhere, and pulled the doors closed.

Wanda the big black girl tucked her in and said, "Now you're going to have some rest, Miss Lily. You worked hard all your life, and now you're going to get some rest."

How silly they all were to assume because you were old and ugly that you had worked hard. She never did a lick she didn't have to. Mama and Sally did the house things. As a girl she had a fantasy she was like a nose. Exposed and vulnerable, she wanted to go everywhere, sniff everything, but not be touched. She had never liked to touch anything, especially things with handles.

"I'm going to wet the bed," she said.

"No you're not Miss Lily. You gone be a good girl tonight. You ain't gone wet no bed."

Ella the blonde girl came in to help clear things up. She was going to college part-time and said she wanted to be a writer. "Here, I brought you a magazine, Miss Lily," she said. "You can read it tomorrow." She put the *Reader's Digest* on the table by the bed, and pulled the lever underneath to raise the bars around the mattress.

"Now you're going to stay put," she said. "Promise me. We don't want to have to strap you down."

"If they come after me I'll have to fight back. Don't strap down my hands."

"Nobody's coming after you, Miss Lily. We'll be here to see they don't, won't we Wanda?"

"Yes ma'am, we'll be here. Nobody gone bother Miss Lily."

"I know what you'uns do here at night," she said.

They gave her the pill but she kept it under her tongue, and as soon as they were gone she spat it out in the little crinkled cup. Mama once said to her, you take these sulfur tablets for worms, and then gave her a spoonful of honey. But she swallowed the honey and spat the sulfur out in the chicken dustholes behind the house.

"Lily didn't take her pills," Sally sang.

"I did too," she said, and pinched her sister, hard.

IN THE DARK she could hear glasses clinking, and dishes rattling down the hall in the dining area. They passed stealthily outside on thick soles, pushing carts and dumb waiters. How clever they thought they were, fooling the old folks whose families paid so much to keep them here. She meant to catch them at their wickedness and call the police or Reverend Sams, expose them once and for all. Of course the world had become such a place maybe no one cared. At least the law should know what went on at Five Oaks. The nurses and aides thought they could get away with anything, night after night, drinking and laughing with the orderlies and the nightwatchman, and doing who knew what all in the lounge and visiting rooms. That's why they threatened to strap her down again, so she couldn't catch them at it and tell.

There was a clue she had, to the secret night life. Because she never slept in the middle of the night, but lay awake between midnight and four or five A.M., even when she took the pills, she heard the car arrive and leave every night. It parked just in front of her window, and someone got out; then after a few minutes it drove away. Without her glasses she couldn't see the digital clock between her and Maggie's beds, but she was sure it was about three-thirty each time. The first two or three nights she saw the lights on her blinds and heard the engine idling, she had not thought it important. But after the fourth or fifth time she knew something was going on. Trying to get out of bed to investigate she tripped somehow and fell. And the next night they strapped her in. To keep you from breaking your bones, Miss Lily, they said. But she knew better. They were afraid of what she might see if she got out in the hall and to the lounge.

Her roommate Maggie was already asleep, snoring faintly on her pillow. She was almost always asleep, even when she wasn't. Sitting up she would say, "A nice day, yes a nice day." Her eyes were empty as a cow's. I'd rather be dead than that stupid, Lily thought. Maggie's family owned dairy farms out on Mills River, and every Sunday afternoon they came with another gift. The digital clock was one, and the transistor radio with the earphones. But Maggie couldn't use it because she couldn't hear without her hearing aid, and the earphones wouldn't fit over the hearing aid. It lay silent as a bar of soap on the shelf, and Maggie sometimes looked at it with a vague and wondering expression. That's how the nurses wanted her to be too, vague and silent, and asleep every night by seven, leaving them free for their good old times. They had not fooled her for a second.

Rubber soles hissed past outside the door, stopped and returned. They were listening, to see if she was out. She lay utterly still, hoping the bed wouldn't rattle. Her heart was thumping so loud they must be able to hear it. Her body shook with its knocking. That was the way she felt when they played hide-and-seek in the bushes behind the house and along the edge of the pasture hill. Calvin was It, and she ran further than anyone, toward the white pines on top of the hill, and hid between a holly bush and a chinquapin. There were burrs on the chinquapin and stickers on the holly leaves, so she could not move without pricking herself. She stood very still in the dusk and listened as the others yelled 'home free' and smacked the dew-damp ground with their dash. Calvin was getting closer. She heard him parting the limbs of brush, looking behind cedars, saying, "I see something in there." She had caught him looking at her more than once in church and at school, then glancing away as their eyes met. She felt her heart jump and bang against her ribs, and breath tear in her throat and chest. Surely he could hear her heart thump. A holly leaf stuck its thorns into her back, and another pushed through her dress to her thigh. If she moved they stung; if she stood completely still they itched and tickled. As Calvin came around the holly, stepping tiptoe, she felt her chest was going to break apart with its jerking. When he saw her he did not yell at first. They stood for one or two seconds, looking frightened at each other, trembling. Then he put his hands on her, right over her heart's galloping, and pressed her breasts through the cotton, for a second, two, before yelling, "You're It."

THERE WAS GIGGLING in the hallway, and someone said, "Is she under?"

"No, she's faking. I can hear her fidget."

It was Wanda, talking to the big orderly Dan, who lifted people when they had to be taken to the infirmary, or restrained them while the nurses put on the straps.

"I'll just hold the pillow over her face," he said. "No one will know the difference."

"Shhhhh," Wanda said. "It won't be long now."

They snickered, like people trying to hold in seizures of laughter. And she heard them pouring something into a glass. They must be carrying a bottle with them, right out in the hall. If only she could catch them, and then tell Reverend Sams. But if they heard her trying to get out of bed they would restrain her. She must be clever this time.

"Here, have some more of this," Dan said.

"Ooooh, that feels just right." Wanda was over six feet. Big women never seemed to have any sense, especially about men.

"Let's give her a little old shot," Wanda whispered.

"OK, I'll get a needle."

She had to think quick. If they gave her the shot, that would be the end of her plans for this night. She had to fool them, so they'd think she was asleep.

The rubber soles whimpered down the hall. Something popped like a champagne cork. She had never seen a champagne bottle, except in the houses of the rich in Flat Rock where she cleaned, but she knew there was a report when the bottle opened. Or maybe it was a gun they were trying out, firing into the couch cushions or pillows in the recreation room. Guns might call the attention of neighbors. But she remembered Five Oaks was on a hill, in the middle of a field, five miles out of town. No one would hear anything. Everyone was inside watching television. That's why they could hell around all night. The Devil had all the cunning he needed.

The door cracked a little. She closed her eyes so hard, so tight, sparks flew out of the corners.

"She's gone," Ella said.

"No, she may be possuming."

"If she wakes we'll give her a squirt with this." Lily relaxed her eyes just enough to see the big pistol in Ella's hand. It was as long as what Daddy used to call a 'horse pistol', the kind they carried in a holster on their saddles in the Confederate War. The nurse held the revolver in one hand and had her other arm around the big orderly. Their breath filled the room with the smell of liquor and drunken bodies. The light behind them made them standing shadows, outlines of emptiness. As they leaned closer she squeezed her eyes again.

"She'll be all right for a while."

"If I have to knock her out I can."

They backed out the door and pulled it to. She heard something click and then click again. They were locking her in. Even if she stayed awake she could not see them at their meanness.

AFTER CALVIN PUT HIS HANDS on her breasts in the hide-and-seek play, she never let him touch her. He followed, and he watched her, on outings to the creek, on berry pickings, at picnics after church, and in the dark after singing school. He tried to get alone with her, but she pushed him away, and tricked him, and slapped him once. How his big work-rough hands fumbled around in the dark just to touch her hip or shoulder. And she slid away to talk to someone else, or vanished into the woods and returned another way to stand with her Mama and the women.

He started seeing her sister Sally, coming with his lantern after church and walking her home, and stopping by to talk to Daddy or her brothers. He even borrowed his uncle's buggy and took Sally out for rides on Sunday afternoon; and there was talk of marriage. Sally whispered to her at night in the big double bed they shared in the attic, about what Calvin said, about their plans.

"Men get uncomfortable there," she said, "Pushing against the tight cloth of their pants. It's not fair." And they laughed under the covers in the cold darkness.

She took to talking to Calvin again, and watching him. And soon he got confused. She saw the day he knew his confusion the first time, when he came for Sally in the buggy but wanted to talk to her. And to be alone with her. He suggested they all three go for a ride, and, thinking of the tiny buggy seat, Sally understood his confusion. "Why don't you'uns just go alone," she said, looking neither at Calvin nor her little sister. She took off her bonnet, and holding it by the strings, ran to the house.

"We're not going without you," Calvin called.

"Oh, let her go if she wants to sulk."

They did go driving, all the way around Mount Olivet to the singing at Poplar Springs, then down the valley, and back up from the store on the turnpike. Calvin talked without pause, once they got away from the house, and tried to put his arm around her. But she leaned away, and then smiled. And he whipped the horse on again.

But she never went out with Calvin again. He came to the house to ask, but she wouldn't see him. And Sally wouldn't either. Sally never married anyone, and neither did she.

THE DOOR WAS BANGING somewhere down at the other end of the corridor, and they were bringing a truck or tractor, or maybe even a bulldozer, inside. The roar of the engine reverberated through the walls, and the tires crunched on the floor. How could such a machine fit in the hallway? Maybe they planned to knock down the walls and bulldoze over her, and blame it on some accident. They might be too drunk to know what they were doing by now. Her Daddy used to say a drunk man had the Devil in his veins, that Satan was distilled into a bottle of whiskey. It was Old Scratch looking at you through a drunk man's eyes.

Something crashed on the floor, maybe a beam of the building. If they knocked it all down they could blame it on structural failure and claim insurance.

The engine quieted and stayed at an idle. There were more shouts, and someone ran by her door. She heard the eerie sound of liquid being poured out on the floor and spread around. They were dumping gasoline on the wing to set it afire. She could not move more than a wrist, as in a nightmare where you felt buried in invisible sand as danger approached. How would she ever get over the railing and through the locked door, or crawl to the window and break it? The swishing liquid came closer, and someone set a bucket down just outside. They had emptied one and were going back for another. Already the gasoline smell was spreading under her door. There was a growing stain there, giving off a harsh perfume, a chemical ghost she had always loved, when it was orange in a can, breathing a shivery mirage. She thought she was going to throw up the bitter coffee.

They spread as much under her door as they could before lighting it. She'd read of gangsters pouring gasoline under the doors of their victims and blowing up their rooms while they slept. She tried to look through the bars at the pool spreading. It seemed to have reached halfway across the room by now, and was soaking into the carpet. The rug would act as a wick, drawing more from outside and torching up on the bed when it was lighted.

They returned with another bucket and set it outside the door. There was a splash and seethe as the fuel was splashed from wall to wall. They were being thorough. It would be like the hell the preacher had always described, the lake of fire the sinners had to stand in in bare feet, hotter than any furnace or burning hay barn, fire on the eyeballs and fingertips, scorching hair and nostrils and lips, frying and blistering, a storm of flame searing through the face forever, in the infinite pits.

They were in a hurry now, slamming the cans and buckets around, slinging gasoline on the floors and walls. She should be praying, asking forgiveness. She had forgotten about prayer, as she always had, all her life. Someone screamed. Either they had killed another patient, or were torturing an old woman in the other wing. They probably took drugs as well as getting drunk. Ella had a key to the dispensary and could get whatever she wanted. Another scream, and then laughter. She saw the big orderly hovering over one of the nurse's aides. Someone squished down the hall laughing.

They revved the big motor at the end of the hall. The building was T-shaped, and her best hope was they would bulldoze the other wing first. If she had just a little time to plan what to do. Buzzing the front desk would tell them she was awake. She must throw something through the window and climb out that way.

The engine got louder. They were coming directly at her, saving the other wing till later. It sounded like a locomotive crunching down the hall, wrapped in the ermine of its steam and smoke. She tried to raise herself within the rails of the bed, but fell back helpless. She couldn't pray. She could think only of the bad things she had done. From her earliest memory she had been evil. And never had she repented: for catching the mouse in the snow storm and cooking it and telling Sally it was a snowbird—for looking in the keyhole at Mama and Daddy in the moonlight—for keeping her eyes open when all else were praying—for saying she accepted Jesus Christ as her personal Savior when she felt nothing—for splitting up Sarah Ballard and her fiancé and then dropping him, for splitting up Deena Reese and Joe Staton and then dropping him—for flirting with Calvin until he fell in love with her and then dropping him—for being afraid of marriage—for the secret pleasures she knew about at night under the quilts—for the rumors she started about the preacher and her cousin Hortense—for the little things, rings, compacts, handkerchiefs, she had stolen in the dimestore all her life—for not going to church after she knew she was not getting married—for her excuse that she 'had to take care of Mother'—for listening to the preacher when he came by and smiling, not believing a word he said—for cussing to herself and Sally every day of her life and for cutting a rusty when anything went wrong—for her selfishness hiding crackers and cookies when her nieces and nephews came on Sunday afternoons—for taking people's charity money and looking down on them as trash—for her hatred of the North and Yankees for the Civil War and for the South losing—for her hatred of the South—for feeling superior in her poverty to the young and ill-bred with their jobs and cars and families—for her hatred of herself and her dried-up and pointless life. Her sins were being visited on her. Maybe she had already died and was in hell. But she smelled gasoline instead of brimstone. Hell couldn't be any worse than Five Oaks. Would she spend the next ten thousand years thinking of herself in a rest home?

The big tracks were crushing the floor tiles and the blade crumbled wall plaster, studs, overhead beams. Soon the whole wing would collapse. Maybe their plan was to push it all down on top of her and light the gasoline already soaked in. Her arms and feet felt encased in lead, under hundreds of feet of water, with tons of pressure on every square inch of her skin.

Over the roar of the machine she heard somebody singing, "Nearer My God To Thee". They were doing it to tease
her, to make her more afraid with their sacrilegiousness. The
drunken voice slurred half the words, but she heard them
distinctly. The song they played on the Titanic as it went
down. She was twenty then and she had the most beautiful
voice in church. Adjer Pace once told her, long after she was
middle-aged and he was married, with kids, and had quit
drinking, that he came, when a sinner, to sit in the pines
behind the church to listen to her sing. He never came inside,
but waited in all weather just to catch her voice among the
choir of women. Her singing helped bring him to the Lord,
he said.

She hated her vanity, and how she laughed to herself at
the seriousness of his story. People were so solemn they were
all fools and didn't know it.

She wanted to laugh in his face when George her
nephew came to see her. How he put on a mask of concern
to walk into her room and ask how she was, the smell of his
business lunch still on his breath and the wrinkles of laughter
still showing around his mouth. And he would ask if she
knew who this was, when he brought his daughter, and she
said, "I ain't that crazy yet." And he talked loud, as though
she was deaf.

He had gotten her power of attorney, and the right to sell
the place. That's what he was thinking about. How to seem
worried about the old woman, and serious in her presence,
so he knew he was doing his duty, but all the time calculating
his share of the homeplace and the bank account. She hoped
to use up all the money in the rest home, till there was just
enough left to bury her. He'd pick the cheapest coffin and
service anyway.

When Sally died they found in her Bible a twenty dollar
bill between each page. There were more than a thousand
liquor bottles in her closet too, but that was forgotten when
George, going through her Bible, found the money. Between
the tintypes of Grandmother and Grandpappy before they
moved off the mountain, and the cards and notes she had
received at Christmas, and a sepia of Calvin, and snapshots

of the Johnson boys, and the India paper pages, lay the starched twenties, saved from her Social Security, and from selling eggs and cleaning for the rich people at Flat Rock. More than seventeen thousand total. But the six hundred a month for Five Oaks was eating steadily into the account. George hated her for every week she stayed alive.

She had always been spoiled. Her Daddy petted and nussed her, and carried her to church—rumor said—until her feet dragged the ground. He believed what she said. When Sally and her brothers were catching birds in the big snow of '98, they raked a patch of the yard bare with brooms and hoes, and scattered crumbs on the ground. Then they propped a wooden box with a stick of kindling with a string tied to it, and when a bird followed the crumbs under the box they jerked the string and the bird was caught. Their hands got so cold they could hardly feel, reaching under the box for the fluttering things. They rushed, wringing the tiny neck, to the wash cauldron of hot water behind the house, to scald the feathers, same as for plucking a chicken. Plucked and gutted, the little fowl was turned on a switch over the fire and eaten in slivers of sweet flesh.

When Sally wouldn't let her hold the string she got the idea for revenge. It was snowing hard, and she slipped out to the crib where Daddy had set the mouse trap. Sure enough, there was scratching and a scuttle inside the box. With her mittens on to keep it from biting, she reached in for the little rodent and pinched its neck between her fingers until it was still. Holding the mouse in her closed mitten she carried it to the back yard and skinned it as she had seen Daddy and her brothers skin rabbits and squirrels and dress them for frying. Fearing the front legs would not look like wings, she cut them off, and roasted the body over the cauldron fire, while Sally was trying to trap another snowbird.

"We must have scared all the birds away," Sally said, coming back to the fire to warm her hands.

"No we ain't. I just caught one."

"Where?"

"While you was inside."

"I don't believe you caught it yourself."

"I was going to give it to you."

"Yeah, I bet."

But Sally took it and ate it all, in little pieces picked off the tiny ribs, while it was steaming in the snowy air. She watched her finish it and then told her. Sally tried to throw up in the snow, and couldn't, and ran to tell Daddy.

"Sister, is this true?" he said from the doorway.

"Is what true?"

"That you gave Sally a mouse and told her it was a bird."

"I was just teasing her."

"She was not."

"I caught a bird and cooked it and gave it to her."

He always believed her. And Sally never knew what to believe. But after he went back inside she whispered to Sally, "You ate a rat, you ate a rat. At least I never ate no rat."

THE BULLDOZER WAS CRASHING through the plaster, breaking laths, splintering studs and sills. The wall trembled with the impact, and the ceiling shook. Maggie would never know when the walls collapsed on her.

"Is she asleep in there?" somebody called.

"Let her die awake if she wants to."

There was a grinding of the blade on metal, and then the flash of something shorting out. The digital clock by the bed went dark. When the walls fell in on her she might be electrocuted before being crushed. Then she would never feel the burning.

"Now back up and hit again."

The machine roared louder, and rammed into a post, paused a moment, revved again, hitting her door like an avalanche of granite. The hinges tore out on their screws and the bolt of the door bent in its slot.

"This is the end I guess," she said, almost calmly. But her roommate never answered. Maybe she was already dead from the gasoline fumes. There was no way to hear her snoring.

Lily lay rigid in the dark waiting for the walls to hit her face, and the burn of the gasoline flaring from the floor. She wanted to die at home as Mama and Daddy and Sally had.

She was being punished for her iniquity. Every cell in her body trembled with anticipation of pain. She lay alert as a dry leaf on a pool, sensitive to any breeze or current.

But the machine quieted, and seemed to be backing down the hall. Perhaps to gather speed for a last assault. Perhaps they thought she was already dead. Maybe they wanted to burn her alive and then bulldoze over the ashes, claiming she was a victim of their efforts to put out the fire.

Whatever they thought, in their drunken wickedness, they had better take care of her now, once and for all. If by some miracle she survived the night she would not only tell Reverend Sams on them, she would see they were punished down to the last fat orderly and clerk and piss-carrying assistant. Behind her tightly closed eyes she saw them all crawling and drowning in the flames they had meant for her.

The Pickup

Now I'm as fair as the next man and nobody can say I ever mistreated no woman no matter what you may have heard. People will say anything. You know as well as I do people will hear a story and then make it sound worser when they tell it just for fun. I may even have done it myself. You have to be careful who you listen to these days.

When Joe Lamar got out of his truck and walked up to the porch I greeted him as nice as I would any man. But when he said, "You stay away from Mother, Mr. Vance. You come around her again I'll break your bones," you could have knocked me dead with a pipe cleaner. I never held any brief with family fighting and with doing women dirty, and with violence. And now they're saying I don't know what all about me all over the county.

You could ask Lurleen, if she wasn't dead, if I ever hit her or abused her about. And she'd tell you straight off I never laid a hand on her in anger. We had our differences and our arguments as any couple will, but I never went that far. I'm a believer in being in charge, but I've always behaved myself around women.

My daddy always said don't ever let a woman get on top or you'll never be in control again. I stayed on top, I'll tell you, the way God meant a man to, but I was civilized and decent.

These people have always tried to run me out of the community since I was a boy because my people come here late, and because my daddy got sent up for making liquor. Half the people in the county made moonshine during Prohibition, but he got caught and put on the road, and then got whipped for smuggling liquor into the jail. The hypocrites would never treat us fair. That's what the land feud was all about, but I won't go into that.

This mess all started back when Lurleen died and left me on my own. Her cancer sickness wore me out with all the treatments and pain and trips to the hospital in Asheville. They cut her open and put tubes in every hole and pumped in so many chemicals she wasn't herself anymore. Nobody should have to witness such a thing. It made me wonder about God's plan for every life to have to watch such judgment on human flesh.

And all that time them lawyers was going back and forth about the line over the mountain. I had sued the Cantrells for my rightful boundary and they had sued me for trespassing. Their old family line going back to before the Silver War didn't mean a thing since it was in the wrong place. They didn't even know how to survey back then. I found the mistake in the old deed; it was right there clear for anybody to read. I got letters from their lawyers warning me not to cut any more wood on my own land, and threatening me with kingdom come. And I'd see them up town or at church and they wouldn't hardly speak, like they was too good to notice me.

All this time Lurleen was dying on me. And then she did die, weighing no more than sixty pounds at the last. And I was wore out.

Now rich people when they've had troubles or a death in the family will go off on a long trip. I've read about it in magazines. But I didn't have a cent after all those bills was paid, and my pickup was wore out. That's why I started going down to the firehall at the cotton mill every Tuesday, Wednesday and Thursday, just to get out and see people again.

I always said I'd never take no charity for old people. I have pulled my own oar so to speak. But the county has been giving these free lunches for the seniors for several years. I'd heard about how people went down there and ate and talked half the afternoon.

Can't say I didn't know it was a place where widows and widowers would flirt and get together. There was rumors about the romances that sprang up around the lunches and sometimes got continued back at home. But I went there just to free my mind from the memories of Lurleen in her last months.

The county sends a bus up the creek road every day about eleven to pick up the oldsters going to the firehall. I caught it one day in early April, out at the church, and it was a good feeling to be going somewhere. I'd even put on a tie, but nobody else was that dressed up. I felt younger already, riding in that old school bus down to the cotton mill. Us old folks acted like kids again.

I stood up in the aisle to talk to Johnny and Luellen Reece and the driver called back, "No standing while the bus is moving."

I felt so full of cheer I said, "It's all right, I'm a member in good standing."

Everybody in the bus laughed, and the driver laughed too. I sat down across from Johnny and Luellen.

"Not many members in good standing at our age," Johnny said in a low voice, but those close by heard and laughed again.

"Johnny, shame on you," Luellen said.

"I just tell it like it is," he said, red in the face from laughing.

"You can't *stand* to tell it any other way," I said, getting even sillier, and we all laughed again.

It felt like being six years old on the first day of school. We laughed all the way down the creek road. There was a crowd already at the firehall when we arrived.

I don't think I had seen Nettie in forty years, not since she was first married to Hank right after the war, and they come to church with their little boy one Homecoming Sunday. She was the prettiest woman in the class by far at high school. Her black hair was now silver, but her skin looked younger than any sixty-eight, and her features were still perfect. And she had kept her figure better than would seem possible.

"It's mighty good to see you," I said, and kissed her on the cheeks.

"I'm sorry to hear about Lurleen," she said. "Cancer is a terrible thing."

I remembered that I'd heard Hank died of cancer too. After he come back from the Pacific they moved over to Enka where he worked in the chemical plant. Most people that ever worked in chemicals got cancer. I think even smelling the fumes of that place would give you cancer.

"And I was mighty sad to hear about Hank," I said. We embraced and held each other for a few seconds. Hugging has come back into fashion, I'm happy to say. I was gladder than ever that I had come.

"What's rich folks doing back among the poor people?" I said. Nettie always did dress well. Even when we was in school, in the Depression, she looked better dressed than any other girl. She had that ability to make whatever she wore seem stylish, though her folks didn't have any money. Now she looked like a billion in her yellow dress. I hadn't seen anything so pretty in years.

Hank must have made a fortune working all that time at Enka. I heard he went back to school and worked his way up to a supervisor's position. Everything about Nettie looked prosperous.

They brought in the lunches on styrofoam plates, the kind with lids and compartments for the meat and vegetables. I had thought it would be homestyle, where they passed around bowls of everything like we used to. But they fixed the meals in town and brought them down in the van. It had all been planned and measured out by dietitians. And it was stuff chosen for old people, chicken in gravy, creamed corn, raisin muffins.

But I wasn't hardly looking at the food anyway. I sipped my coffee and smiled at Nettie. And she smiled back, all poised and proper, the way she always was.

"Are you going to Florida this fall?" Luellen said to her.

"I may," Nettie said. "Joe Lamar says he'll drive me down, and Mildred, Hank's sister, says I can stay with them."

"You don't want to leave here," I said, glad my plate had stayed in when I bit down on a sliver of chicken bone. "You want to stay among friends."

"I wish we could afford to just up and go to Florida," Luellen said.

"Florida's a place to go for honeymoons and vacations," I said. "It's no place to live." I found myself talking proper English around Nettie.

"It's good not to have to worry about the snow or falling on ice," Johnny said.

When they brought more coffee to the tables I looked at Nettie and said, "It's awful good to see you in these parts again."

"Good to be back," she said.

"Have you been up to the old place?" Luellen said.

"No, but I'd love to see it. Joe Lamar said he would drive me by there one day."

"You won't recognize it," Johnny said. "They've put siding on the house, and all the pasture and fields are divided up in lots for trailers. Larry Dean's making him a development."

"It's too bad Mama had to sell the place," Nettie said. "Still, I'd like to see it."

"Well let's go see it," I said. "It's such a pretty day. You ride back on the bus with me and we'll take my truck. I'll drive you up the mountain."

"But Joe Lamar will wonder what happened to me," Nettie said.

"I can take you back to his place before he even gets home from work."

So she agreed. And friends, let me tell you, that was one

of those afternoons you spend your whole life waiting for. The sun was bright but it wasn't too hot. I wasn't even too embarrassed by my old truck. I pushed some rags and tools out of the way and wiped off the seat. Nettie in her bright yellow dress looked like spring itself.

We drove up the creek where they were setting out sweet potato plants in the new-plowed fields. The mountain tops were still bare, but trees along the creek were putting out yellow and gold. By midafternoon you could hear the peepers calling from wet places along the creek.

"They're hollering for mates," I said. "It's a love call that you're hearing." Nettie smiled, and I took her hand until I had to shift down or stall out as we started up the mountain.

"I had forgotten how beautiful it is up here," she said.

We stopped by the spring below Raven Rock and drank from the coffee can somebody had left there on a stick.

You know how it is when you're with somebody you care about. Everything seems different and perfect. The way the light fell through the trees, and the way the mountains in the distance looked, seemed part of our happiness. That old road across the mountain wasn't a bit too long for once. I didn't want to arrive, and I didn't want the afternoon to end. I shifted down to low and whined over the summit, and then crept down over the washouts and switchbacks. A pheasant ran across the road in front of us.

"That's a good omen," Nettie said.

"A what?"

"Something nice." She smiled.

"WHY LAW," Nettie said as we rolled down the cove and came out into the open, at the edge of what was her daddy's place. She lowered her window to look, as I slowed, until our dust caught up with us.

Part of the pasture fence was still intact, but the barbed wire zigzagged from posts leaning one way to posts leaning the other. Where the fence ran along the branch the water had undercut some of the posts, and they hung on the wires midair. The pasture was mostly briars and young bastard pines.

"Why law," Nettie said again. But she wasn't looking at the pasture and fields by the branch. She had already seen the hill pasture beyond the house. Shelves had been bulldozed in the red clay all the way up the ridge and a few trailers had already been moved into them.

But it wasn't the trailers only that made the hill look so bad. It was the great piles of trees that had been pushed to the edge of the clearing and left, and the spills of red dirt down the slope below the shelves. Roads had been cut winding around the old pasture hill. And the March rains had washed everything so each shelf had bled through the weeds down to the next. Even the grass below was red and ugly.

"The law," Nettie said. I stopped in front of the house. The old hedge had been cut down and a new carport built beside the driveway.

"You want to go in?" I said. "We could ask them."

Nettie shook her head, and I drove on.

"The only thing clean on the hill is the new satellites," I said.

"They look like mushrooms coming out of the red clay."

The dust caught up with us again, and I was going to speed up, but Nettie pointed to a spot by the bend, hidden in rhododendron. "Let me see the old spring," she said.

I parked and we worked our way down the weedy bank into the laurels. I helped her on the steep place, putting my hands on her waist which was slim as a girl's.

"The old spring was right here," she said. "We used to stop here for a drink after getting off the school bus at the forks."

When we found it the spring was covered with briars, and mud from the bulldozing above had washed into its pool. There was a red silt lining on the basin, and leaves were piled up around the outlet.

"This was the best tasting water I ever had," she said. "But I guess that's just nostalgia playing tricks." She laughed, and I helped her up the bank.

I drove on down to the forks of the road.

"This is where we used to wait for the school bus," she said. "It was so cold we got numb some mornings."

"That's how I remember you, arriving in your red coat with your cheeks all flushed by cold." I took her hand. "You were the prettiest thing I had ever seen."

"We were just kids," she said.

"I've always been sweet on you. And I'm still a man with love feelings," I said.

"Through Hank's long illness I didn't ever think I could feel love again."

"I know what you mean. Watching Lurleen waste away seemed to kill something in me. Even though I was a strong and healthy man, if you know what I mean."

Nettie smiled and squeezed my hand. "You remind me of the good times," she said.

We reached the paved road and I headed for town. "I believe in talking honest with a woman," I said. "It's no good holding back. I'm a man of strong feelings, just as much as when I was young."

"Who would have guessed when we were in high school that we would feel this way when we were grandparents," she said.

"I've got a lot of life left in me yet."

We were coming into town. I hated to see the drive nearing its end.

"Joe Lamar's house is out on Highland Road," she said. "Just go on past the reservoir."

"Living in the rich part of town."

"He's done well with his company."

I turned into the driveway and a little dog run up to the truck and barked.

"Get down Kinder," Nettie said.

"I hope to see you again."

"I'll go down to the firehall again, soon."

"How soon."

"Tomorrow."

As I DROVE HOME I knew what I would say to her the next time. I would tell her it was time to think about who we wanted to end with. That we had been given another chance to be together and should not lose it. That in the years left we should bring each other happiness. And when I took her for a ride the following week I did say those things, when we parked on top of Pinnacle Mountain. And she cried when I kissed her.

Now I'm the kind of man that when he has something on his chest will out with it. I never was any good at holding back when the truth was there to tell. It never did anybody any good to run around pretending. And I'm here to tell you I wasn't treated fair.

"It shouldn't be in the church," she said.

"Why not?" I said, though I was really relieved.

"Well at our age, and for the second time, it wouldn't seem appropriate."

"I'll marry you wherever you say."

"Joe Lamar's house would be cheapest. We could have the reception there too." A frown must have passed across my face. With all that money Hank had made I didn't see why she would worry about the expense of the reception.

"We could have it at the firehall, at lunchtime," I said. "That way all our friends could be there."

"That's the best idea yet," she said and smiled.

And then we got to talking about honeymoons, and trips to Gatlinburg or Myrtle Beach.

"We could to go to Florida and visit Mildred, and see Silver Springs," she said.

"I don't know if my old truck would make it to Florida," I said. "It's getting long in the tooth, unlike me." We laughed.

"You can have Hank's pickup," she said. "It's an almost new GMC. We were going to sell it, but now you can have it."

I have always wanted a GMC, and this seemed like a surprise present. She had never mentioned it before.

"He got it the year before he got sick," she said. "To haul his little tractor up to the farm he bought north of Weaverville."

I didn't say any more, but if it was possible to be happier than I was before, I was. A new GMC truck, a tractor, and a farm north of Weaverville, as well as Nettie. Things was coming right for me for the first time in fifty years. Maybe I could pay a lawyer to settle the land dispute, or at least we could move away from the aggravation. I prayed to God he'd let me live long enough to enjoy this change of fortune.

"Joe Lamar wants to talk with you," Nettie said.

"Fine, I'll be glad to talk with him," I said.

"Just to settle up the business stuff. He has all the papers and all the details."

"That's fine," I said, and took her in my arms.

Joe Lamar called and asked me to meet him at his office in town the next day. He runs a small construction company that specializes in repair work and renovating, and his office is just a room above the paint store on Mitchell Street. I don't think he even has a secretary. It was just him at a desk with coffee stains and papers, with a Xerox machine in the corner.

"Please have a seat, Mr. Vance," he said.

I sat in front of the desk. I never did like offices. They make you feel like a kid in school who has been called in to see the principal. I can't wait to get outside again.

"We're all pleased that Mother is getting married," he said. "She's had a hard time, and it's what she needs, to get on with her life."

"She's a fine woman," I said.

"I want to go over some of the financial details, so we can work things out fairly for all concerned."

"Fine," I said. "Just fine."

"I don't know how much Mother has explained to you," he said, leaning forward on the desk. "But my father was sick a long time, and ran up a lot of bills, both in Asheville and in Atlanta."

"But he had insurance," I said.

"He did have insurance, but that covered only part of the expenses. Because he owned both the house in Enka and the farm north of Weaverville, he was not eligible for a lot of state and federal aid."

"He must have had savings," I said. "After all the years at Enka."

"He did," Joe Lamar said. "But the year before he got sick he invested most of what he had in stocks. Stocks were booming then. And then he lost that in the crash of 1987.

I waited for him to continue. A firetruck screamed by on the street.

"The truth is the farm in Weaverville and the house and the pickup as well must be sold to pay the bills."

"How much was the bills?" I said.

"About five hundred and fifty thousand dollars for the surgery, the radium treatments, and the chemotherapy, and the stay in intensive care. The two weeks at Emory alone were over a hundred thousand dollars."

I just shook my head. I was glad they had not gone to such lengths for Lurleen.

"The good news is that when the house and farm and truck are sold, everything the insurance doesn't cover will be paid except about seventeen thousand dollars. Maybe as much as twenty-five. But the bulk will be taken care of."

"Who will pay that?" I said.

"Mother will have to. You and she will have to. And I'll help out when I can."

I just walked out of there. He was telling me I had to pay twenty-five thousand dollars just for marrying Nettie. And I had just settled up Lurleen's bills and didn't have a cent left over, even to fix my truck. All I had was social security. As I drove home I got madder by the mile. Nettie had not even told me there were debts. All she had mentioned was the GMC and the tractor which she would give to me. I drove straight to Joe Lamar's house. I never was one to hold in something.

But turning into the driveway I didn't see the garbage cans somebody had put at the entrance. Maybe I need my glasses changed. First think I knew the bumper banged on the two cans and garbage shot out all over the street like it had been kept under pressure.

I got out and was trying to pick up the mess of bags and coffee filters and styrofoam scattered while several cars paused and honked at me.

"Asshole," somebody yelled from a red Camaro, as they went around.

Nobody talks to me like that. I got back in the truck, which was still running, and headed after the red car. But they were long gone. When I got to the junction of Highland Road and Route 28, there was nothing red in sight except a Volkswagen.

Slow down Will, slow down, I said to myself. My hands were shaking on the wheel. I could turn around and go back to Joe Lamar's and tell Nettie what I thought, or I could go on home. My blood pressure was getting up, but I was never one to hold something in. I'd turn around and go back to Joe Lamar's.

Cars was honking behind me, and I realized the pickup had gone dead. I turned the key, but it would not catch. I turned it again and again, but nothing helped. Meantime the truck had rolled part way out into Route 28 and cars were having to swerve into the next lane to go around. I was being blown at from two directions. I turned the key until my finger hurt.

"Mister." The man behind me had come around to my window. "Mister, it's just flooded. Push the gas pedal all the way down and turn it again."

Well I knowed that as well as he did, but I wasn't thinking. I pushed in the accelerator and the old truck caught, popping and rumbling from too much gas, but its pulse picked up, and blue smoke poured out the back. It was too late to turn back toward Joe Lamar's, so I threw it into gear and headed into the highway. My hands were still shaking, and I thought I'd go to the firehall to have some coffee and decide what to do.

It was a little too late for lunch, but I parked beside the van and went inside. And by God there was Nettie sitting with Luellen and Johnny and all the rest of them. They all spoke to me, and I nodded, trying to keep calm. I didn't want to have no stroke. I just went to the coffee urn to get a cup. But my hands must have been shaking still for the full cup just seemed to fly out of my fingers and spray all over the floor.

"Oh Will," Nettie said, and came over to help wipe it up.

"So I can have the new pickup?" I said. I was never good at talking angry. She looked at me in surprise.

"If I'm willing to pay twenty thousand dollars," I said.

"Don't say it like that," she said, "Here, with everybody listening."

"You picked the wrong man," I said. "I've done paid the doctors everything I have."

I left the coffee half mopped up, and I got out of there, with everybody looking. I just brushed by her, though Joe Lamar said I pushed her. I did no such thing. She may have grabbed my arm and I just pulled away. But I didn't push anybody. I got in my truck and drove straight home. They'll tell all over the cotton mill I hit her, or I pushed her, or I slapped her, but there's not a word of it true.

That's why I was so shocked when Joe Lamar came driving up into my yard and said not to never see his mother again. Like I had been the one to do something wrong. They act like I was the guilty party. I'll tell anybody the truth if they ask me.

Somebody even said they had the preacher criticizing me behind my back. I ask you, what kind of fair is that? And people at the firehall talking about me jilting Nettie and making her cry. What do they care about my disappointment?

One time when I was a boy my brother Charles and me give Mama all our money to save while we worked in the pulpwood. She kept it in two jars somewhere in the house. Now I made more than Charles because I worked longer days, and carried my wood all the way to Canton to sell directly to the plant. So I know good and well I had to have more money than Charles did. But when it come time before Christmas for her to give us our savings, it turned out we had the same thing in both jars.

Charles must have found where she hid the jars and put some of my money in his, for that's the only way to explain it. I never did accuse Mama of evening the jars, though she always took Charles's side. After all he was the little brother. She said he had worked just the same as me. There was nothing fair about it.

Mama said, "How do you *know* how much was in your jar? Maybe Brother Charles made extra money you don't know about selling Christmas greens."

I could see I was beat from the start. Everybody had decided in Charles's favor, and I was the one robbed. I kept my own money after that in a coffee can out behind the spring house.

With people talking that way I don't even want to go to church no more. I don't even want to drive up in the mountains to see the rhododendrons and the flame azaleas. And they can keep their lunches in styrofoam, and the silly talk of old people flirting down at the firehall. I've ordered a thousand hemlocks from the government to set out by the branch. They'll be worth ten dollars apiece in a few years. Another idea I have is turning my land into a trailer park. I've got enough water and acres to do it. Let's see what the Cantrells and everybody else has to say about that.

Blinding Daylight

HE WAS TRYING to find his mother's pistol. It was a little .22 caliber revolver which she had kept under some clothes in the chest of drawers. She had always urged him to carry it when he went into the woods. "You might see a snake," she would say, "There's been rattlers all over the mountain." Or, "There's been reports of wild dogs out, you better carry this." And later, when he returned home from his first teaching job: "There's hippies in the mountains now, crazy with drugs and liable to do anything. I'd not go back there unless I was armed."

A dozen times he carried the little .22 in his coat pocket and never fired it once. Those had been peaceful saunters and climbs back into the woods he had hunted as a teenager. They had been walks of pleasure and therapy. Once he had been so distraught in graduate school he could neither paint nor sleep, worrying he would be drafted. Should he vanish to Canada? Shoot off a toe? Join the Air Force? He took the bus home and walked out his frustration in the mountains. Standing on the ridge of Hogback, ankle-deep in new-fallen leaves, he had gotten his first really good idea. As soon as he was back in Durham he started the "Ocean of Mountains" series, of ridges cresting one behind the other like successive tidal waves bearing down on the viewer. That group of paintings had got him his MFA degree, his first one-man show in Charlotte, his first two sales, and a teaching job at Piedmont State University. Even though he was 1-A he had never been drafted. Too many boys in his county who had not gone to college, who had not even gone to high school for that matter, were available for Vietnam.

He pushed aside some old photographs in the second drawer. The picture on top must have been snapped by him: a family group, Christmas 1968. His first wife stood by his parents at the fireplace. There were decorations on the mantel behind them, including turkey's paw gathered under the pines on the north side of the pasture hill. The following March he came back alone at spring break, sick with love for another woman, a dance teacher at the college where he had gone after Piedmont. He thought of suicide as he carried his mother's revolver on a long walk back to Grassy Creek and the Flat Woods. Two things were clear to him: if he was going to do it, he must do it away from anybody's house, so there would be no mess, no children frightened, and he must do it where he felt most at home, in the haze and tree-breath of the high mountains. Above the Briggs Place he stopped at an abandoned field that might at one time have been under polebeans. Now it was broomsedge swaying blond in the midday glare. An old Ford, its windows and headlights broken, rusted on its axles blocking the only access road to the remote clearing. Later he fancied a number had been painted on the door, but he couldn't be certain. The next day, back in Virginia, he began a wide painting of a wheatfield with a stock car hovering over it. The field was a million candles of fountaining light, each painted distinctly, and the race car a rush of thunder. Later he realized the secret inspiration must have come from Dali's "Last Supper," as well as the field at the edge of the Flat Woods. The first articles written about him were on the wheatfield and race car paintings. He kept working through that spring and summer until he had more than a hundred canvases. One critic said the power was in the contrast between the ancient and the modern, and quoted Henry Adams from "The Dynamo and the Virgin." Another saw evidence of a schizoid attraction to both gentleness and violence at once. Only the columnist for the Atlanta paper saw a feeling for the miraculous, a retelling of the Ascension, power transcendent to nature.

The pistol was under a framed picture of flowers. It was a cheap print that might have been cut from a magazine. But his mother must have thought it special enough to buy a dimestore frame for it. He tried to remember where it might have hung, either in the old house down by the river or here. The faded dahlias did not seem familiar.

The revolver had a delicate embroidery of rust on the barrel. She had never oiled or cleaned it, as his father did all his guns and rifles. For the first time he realized it was surprising the pistol was here at all. His brother had taken all the hunting rifles and shotguns, and the .44 Ruger his father carried on bear hunts as a backup. He must not have found the .22.

The house smelled horribly and sweetly of mildew. Unlived in, buried in oak shade, the rooms were flanneled and cushioned with mold that seemed to sparkle even in the weak light. His brother and sister-in-law had taken all the living room furniture, but had left the kitchen intact, hoping to rent the house partly furnished to summer people. His parents' bedroom they left because the suit was so old, its veneer cracking.

He opened the cylinder and saw that all nine chambers were still loaded. She must have kept it ready, after his father died and she was alone, for any burglar or crazed hippy unlucky enough to try her door. There were specks of blue corrosion on the little cartridge heads, but he was sure they would still fire. In any case, he had stopped at the Western Auto for a new box of ammunition.

He saw himself in the dresser mirror as he clicked the cylinder back in place, and quickly looked away.

Joan had not protested when he told her he was coming back. Since she would need the car to get to her job, and to take the children to violin and gymnastics lessons, he decided to fly. His spring vacation and the children's never seemed to coincide anyway.

"You go down for a few days," she said. "The rest will help and you always get your best ideas there." She had ironed and packed his shirts and pants, and made sure his hiking boots were included. She pretended not to notice when he was too tired for lovemaking, and showed enthusiasm when he did feel the need.

He laid the revolver down on the dusty bed and looked into the top drawer. Most of the albums and pictures his mother kept there had been taken. There were scattered snapshots that no one wanted, of army buddies of his uncles standing in front of Quonset huts, and portraits in stiff cardboard frames of relatives no one could remember. There were letters he had written from college which she had saved, a few clippings about his early fellowships and shows. After he had the first opening in New York she seemed to lose interest. Perhaps she felt out of touch with something so distant. She had given almost the only encouragement, in the desperate days of college and graduate school, when the family laughed at him for dropping out of engineering. But she appeared to actually resent it when he began to be known. In the last years, after his father's stroke, she had hardly shown a perfunctory interest in his new work, in the reviews and sales. Compensation, he thought. For every gain you lose something equally precious.

Until his father's sickness he had never thought much about hospitals, insurance, rest homes. Suddenly the man who had been so strong, so hardworking, was a heavy child to be cajoled and appeased, to be lifted and taken to the toilet. The first time he visited the rest home he had been sick in the grass by the parking lot. The smell of alcohol, of medicine, of urine and disinfectant, was suffocating. It was the smell of corridor after corridor, of the old in wheelchairs, watching TV, staring into the dim light, waiting. His father had tears in his eyes from the pain. The stroke made him weep unexpectedly and uncontrollably, his mother said. It didn't mean anything. But he was also in pain.

"My daddy needs a shot," he told the nurse.

"The doctor has a strict schedule," she said. "It's not time for medication yet."

He had never heard of pain from a stroke before. It had something to do with the nerve impulses being blocked, he was told.

"Just bring in my .44 magnum and shoot me," his father said.

"Sickness changes one mentally," the doctor told him. "No sickness is just of the body. You'll have to allow for that. You see the world from a different angle in sickness. It's as though the picture of your life has been foreshortened and everything in the composition is rearranged slightly."

The doctor was from Brazil, but he had an Italian name and almost no accent. Knowing David was a painter he talked about cultural things.

"My favorite American author was Ambrose Bierce in college," he said while watching the sphygmomanometer. "His stories of the macabre were the best I ever read."

"He vanished into Mexico and was never found, I believe."

"That's a daydream we all entertain at times," the doctor said, writing on his clipboard. "To disappear like Shakespeare's Ariel into thin air."

His brother had kept the yard in reasonably good shape, in preparation for renting the house. No work had been done on the shrubbery or flowerbeds his mother had made so painstakingly, but the lawn had been raked at least once since fall. Of course, the oaks kept shedding brown leaves right up until the new leaves came out, and several piles could be gathered off the grass.

One of the pleasures of coming South in winter was the way the afternoons warmed up even on the colder days. The sun sparkled on the fallen leaves and silver of bare branches. The ground of the driveway was thawing, and because it was not packed, showed the tracks of the Reliant he had rented at the airport. He checked his pockets; the keys were still in the car.

On a clear March afternoon like this things seemed to trickle and crackle on the southern exposure. The banks that had been whiskered with ice were crumbling, and the maples were red with thousands of match head buds. He had always meant to paint that red misty look they had at a distance. With the trout season just a few weeks away the creeks were bursting with the rush of runoff and rainbow flashes in the shoals. The river was supposed to be too polluted now for trout, but the feeder creeks still got stocked in late winter.

He took his timber cruiser jacket from the back seat of the Reliant and put the pistol in the side game pocket. His hands were steadier than they had been for weeks.

His painting had been more affected than he realized or would admit. It showed first in the close brushwork. In the old days, when he was doing the wheatfields, he could paint for weeks on a square foot of canvas, getting each of the heads of grain right, the seeds and husks and beards on hundreds of individual stalks painted in meticulous detail, in the foreground. And then he gradually made them smaller as they receded toward the horizon. But he kept each head distinct, so the closer a viewer looked the more he saw. He had discovered the Persian miniatures in Washington, and he wanted that kind of biting focus. He trimmed the finest brushes down until they had only half a dozen hairs, and sometimes he used a magnifying glass to get the blades in the distance crisp. He wanted a composition rhythmic and dynamic as Van Gogh's, yet detailed as a reconnaissance photograph under a microscope. He spent weeks looking at rye and wheatfields around Blacksburg, and tried to show how the grain crossed and recrossed heads in a breeze, how at a certain stage in spring the stalks looked metallic, of brushed steel, and then had a band of purple just below the heads as ripening began. After the long sessions painting whiskers and flowerets, and flow-shadows within the acres of long grass, he had headaches that lasted for days. Only love-making would stop the pain, he told his first wife, and they spent afternoons on the mattress on the floor of the near-empty old house.

The story about Berryman came back to him again. The poet's former wife said he used to stand for hours on balconies looking down until she would lead him away. A witness on the bridge in Minneapolis saw him climb over the railing and wave as he fell. But he had read somewhere else that another witness had seen Berryman look back startled, as he fell toward the frozen river, as though realizing he did not want to die yet.

His roommate had been a fan of Hemingway and liked to talk about tests of courage. "They say people who kill themselves are cowards," he liked to observe. "But it takes guts to step off that ledge, or pull that trigger. Hem's greatest testimony was putting that shotgun in his mouth." How boring such judgments had become.

He took the trail down by the field and across the pasture. Since his father's death the land had been rented to neighbors and cousins. They broke up the ground and put in sweet pepper and eggplant crops, but the fields always looked roughly kept. The margins had grown up in big weeds and scrub pine. No one even mowed the edges and the haulroads anymore. There were fertilizer sacks, broken hampers, and papers from McDonald's blown up against the fence.

The pasture had long since gone to thorn and bastard pine. The horse had been sold during his last year of college and the lot had not been grazed since. But under the scrubgrowth and briars he could still discern the sunken trails the cows had walked for a century, and he saw the post that held the block of salt like a popsicle greened by the grass on the cows' tongues.

He would like to have climbed Big Hoot Owl, to the fat poplar on its knob which he had visited on every trip home before. But he was not in good enough shape; the walking had already made him trembly. Perhaps he had had too much coffee on the plane. The old cowpath by the branch had washed into a ditch that was deepening in places to a gully. The branch itself piped along under over-arching weedstalks. Erosion had undercut the fence post and it hung by two barbed strands over the stream. He looked for signs of the dam he and his brother had made, but saw no traces of the days of shovelling that had impounded a swimming hole for all of one summer.

It pleased him to imagine he would never have to attend faculty meetings and discuss budgets again, never chair another committee. He would not serve as a judge for Guggenheims anymore, nor evaluate graduate applications. He would never go to a dentist again, nor negotiate with a car salesman, nor wait at a garage, nor write up a talk on the relationship of his painting to the South. He would never have to move his studio again, nor talk to a gallery owner, nor appear at an opening and chat with buyers. He would not have to worry about tuition payments, nor about what aging does to the body, to the power of color discrimination, to the accuracy of the brush hand.

He wished he had brought a radio, or better still a cassette player with some Bach or Richard Strauss. No, that would be too precious. Take whatever comes out of the air: country music, hits from the fifties. The music that occurs.

He crossed the pasture where the ruins of the molasses furnace had been scattered when he was a boy. His grandfather and great-grandfather had boiled syrup there every fall since the Confederate War. Their horses had circled thousands of times in the autumn, crushing the juice from the big grass stalks. There was nothing but a slight indentation where the boiler had been. He passed the house place where he had lived until the age of four and the level where the original log barn had stood. His mother as a young woman had taken him and his brother for walks and little picnics along the edge of the hill pasture to the river. She liked to show them bird nests in the blackberry thickets, and sit for hours by the stream, away from the hot canning kitchen and churn and washpot.

There was a large hickory on the hill above the old orchard. It was almost surrounded now by a young pine grove and he could just see out over the valley. He was out of breath and sweating, and sat down at the tree base, leaning against the rough bark. The damp came quickly through the leaves to the seat of his pants. He thought about moving, but laughed at himself. This was the only place, besides his studio, he had ever felt truly at ease. Flies and yellow jackets were crawling on the leaves around him. They must have wintered in the mulch of the dirt and the warmth had brought them out into the blinding sunlight. He saw a hickory nut the squirrels had missed, against a stick, and wondered if the meat was still good.

The sunlight made the dry leaves shine on the slope, the silver bark and trees, the stubbled fields and creek, and the ruins of the old log barn where his grandmother had seen Halley's Comet glistened as though polished, growing brighter and signalling as he blinked. He closed his eyes, and when he opened them the separate shapes and distances burned harder, merging in a flood, a storm advancing over him.